Gian

THE DELGADO TRILOGY

NATALIA LOUROSE

Playlist

WE MUST BE KILLERS, MIKKY EKKO
FIGHTING DEMONS, JUICE WRLD
NO ONE'S IN THE ROOM, JESSE REYEZ
FINALLY // BEAUTIFUL STRANGER, HALSEY
PEACE, TAYLOR SWIFT
HOMICIDE LOVE, JAMES ARTHUR
MAD WOMAN, TAYLOR SWIFT
I CAN'T BREATH, BEA MILLER
DARKEST HOUR, ANDREA RUSSETT
FEEL, FLETCHER
YEARS TO GO, G EASY AND GOODY GRACE
THE BEAUTIFUL AND THE DAMNED, G EASY
I SEE RED, EVERYBODY'S AND OUTLAW
YOU DON'T OWN ME, SAYGRACE AND G EASY
DEVIL I KNOW, ALLIE X
CRUEL INTENTIONS, DELACEY AND G EASY

TO ANYONE THAT HAS EVER FELT TRAPPED-
I DON'T KNOW WHO MADE Y
OU FEEL LIKE YOU WERE'NT ENOUGH,
WHO SAID YOU COULDN'T CHANGE,
AND GROW, AND FLY.
BUT HEAR ME WHEN I SAY:
THY WERE WRONG.

THIS ONE'S FOR YOU.

OUR MOTHER TELL US THAT
THERE ARE NO MONSTER
UNDER OUR BEDS,
OR HIDDEN IN OUR CLOSETS,
BUT THEY DIDN'T WARN US
THAT SOMETHINGS MONSTERS
COME DRESSED AS PEOPLE
THAT CLAIM TO LOE YOU
MORE THAN THE SUN
LVES THE MOON.

-Nikita Gill

Gian

Chapter One

GIAN

The smell of death infiltrates my nostrils, burning into my senses. My gag reflex disappeared long ago, there's no place for sickness in this world. Instead, I hold in my nausea, clenching my squirming stomach.

The offensive odor comes from the corpse in front of me, his fresh death still lingering in the air. Blood streams down the plastic tarp like a gelatinous gravy flowing from his multiple wounds.

I shift my focus from the rotting body, from the man who used to be my friend, unable to focus on his face anymore.

There's blood on my sleeve. I scratch at the spot, which only serves to spread the liquid, staining the shirt further. All my attention goes to the crimson speck.

"Do you have an extra shirt?" I ask my brother, whose own white shirt is spotless as he leans against the brick wall of the warehouse, typing away on his cell phone. He looks up when I speak, his eyes roaming over me.

"No," he says, pushing himself off the wall. "And yours looks fine."

I extend the offending arm with its spot of blood. It takes my brother a moment before he finally sees it and shakes his head, "You're being crazy."

"Fuck you." I shoot back.

Gio rolls his eyes. "I called the clean-up crew." He tells me, tucking the cell phone back into his pocket. People have always said my little brother looks like me, which is because we have matching heads of dark hair and olive-toned skin, but I don't see it. Gio differs completely from me. A scrap of hair covers his chin where mine is smooth and clean. His nose rounds at the edges where mine is sharp and straight. He wears nothing but jeans and a distressed leather jacket, and I have a closet full of designer suits. We may have the same blood running through our veins, but me and my brother are far from the same.

And maybe it's better that way, maybe that's why we get along so well.

I nod an appreciative thank you to Gio. That's the one decent thing about having power, I no longer have to clean up my own messes, a small blessing. I'm not sure I could wrap up Silvio's body if I had to. I've disposed of many bodies in my fifteen years

12

of being a made man, but Silvio is the first made man I've had to kill.

I slide the cuff links back into place on the dirty shirt and slip my suit jacket on. Unlike my brother, I like to look presentable at all times. Even though the spot is tiny and it's covered by my jacket, I can feel it there. It's searing my arm, tainting my suit jacket. I feel dirty.

It doesn't help that my head is woozy from the kill, my composure is slipping. I don't like to be out of control, and this moment feels far out of my control.

"You need to stop getting your hands dirty." Gio tells me, tilting his head to the body laying on the plastic sheet in the middle of my warehouse, well technically not my warehouse as I don't put places like this in my name. Grabbing his leather jacket off a chair and slipping the thing back onto his shoulders, he gives me a pointed look when I don't respond right away. He means figuratively, not literally, like the stain on my shirt.

This is an ongoing conversation between me and my brother. My father also doesn't stop putting his two cents in on the matter. "I know." I try to shake off the comment, not caring to repeat this conversation.

"Do you?" Gio raises a single eyebrow in question. "Because, if you did, you'd stop."

I know they're right. I need to stop getting my hands dirty, distance myself from the underbelly of the organization. Dirty fingers get men like me caught. The less I kill, the less that's in my name—the better off I'll be. But that's easier said than done.

New to the boss's seat, I'm still gaining the trust of my men. Men who see me as the small boy they watched grow up instead of the man I became. I need to prove myself to them and having the FBI on my tail and a rat in my organization is not helping my mission.

A strangled breath leaves my lips, I straighten out my suit jacket and press my palm down my slacks. My brother is the only one who I allow to grate on my nerves like this. I don't like to show emotion; I like to keep a calm demeanor and with most people I'm able to. Not with Gio. I think he knows me too well to fall for it, anyway. "He was a rat." I fling a hand at the offender, now bloodied and dead on the cement floor.

"Yeah," Gio mumbles, glancing at the man. A kill is never a simple thing, and my brother's face shows his remorse. He'd school his features better if there were other men here. But because it's just us, we can speak freely.

"He was a rat," I say again, this time more for me than my brother. "And he was our Famiglia, so it's my job to take care of him. No one else's." I feel the anger rise in my chest, it's a red heat that bubbles up from my stomach, higher and higher until it reaches my heart. I take a deep breath, silently counting in my head until my heart rate slows and my breathing is even.

One.

Two.

Three.

He was a fucking rat. The one thing you can't be in this life. He took a blood oath, swore an allegiance, yet still he talked to the Feds. I scrub a hand over my face, running over the stubble that I've yet to shave. I feel ten years older since taking over La Famiglia.

But I never wanted another job. This is my place in life.

"If you tell me," I point a finger at my brother, "that he is the last one, then I won't get my hands dirty. But if he's not," I sigh, "then I will paint this town red."

My father's law office is an ugly place. Stuck in the '70s, it boasts old stained carpeting and beige walls. He has plenty of money, and yet he still doesn't upgrade. If you ask him about it, he'll wave a hand dismissively and the corner of his mouth will curve into a scowl. "Ah," he'll say. "It's fine."

A deep smoky scent attacks me when I swing open the glass door. The cigar smell is an alert to my father's presence. Cancer wrapped in brown paper hangs from his lips daily. He swears if cancer hasn't got to him yet, it's not coming. But secretly, I think he'd be fine with dying if it meant seeing Ma again. He won't kill himself though, he's not that kind of man, but he's not taking any precautions either.

But I'm not here to see him.

Instead, I came to visit my baby sister. Gemma's desk is empty, kind of like her presence in my life lately. She's been avoiding me for a while now, since she started fucking around with her now husband. The Irish prick whose bed she frequents.

I feel the anger rising again, red bubbles staining my vision. I revisit my breath, pulling it in to a count of four and exhaling it out to a count of six. A technique gathered off the internet to quell my anger issues. Thinking of Gemma and Liam always seems to spike the demon inside of me, the angrier version of me.

I didn't want her to marry the man. If I had any say they would have never met, but she claims it's true love. Not that I believe in such a silly concept. At the end of the day, my father supports her and Liam, and we made a deal that brought peace between our families.

I still hate the idea of them together, but I'm trying. For her.

I exhale as I glance around. The open office space is empty, both Gemma's and Edie's desks abandoned.

"Can I help you?" I'm too focused on the legs of the voice to move my gaze upwards and see who it is. She's poised in the entryway of the second office in the law firm, the one my father never filled, the one that has sat empty waiting for me.

Not anymore.

The girl is slim and olive-skinned with legs that go for miles, feet fitted in a pair of red Louboutins. She's wrapped tightly in a black pencil skirt with a cream silk top tucked into it. There's a mane of thick, wild, black curls on top of her head, and I have the sudden urge to wrap that hair around my fist and watch the curve of her neck when I pull it taut.

She clicks her tongue and crosses her arms over her chest, crushing the paper she's holding in the process. "Can I help you?"

She asks again, this time her voice is deep and stern.

I raise an eyebrow as a smirk grows on my face. People don't challenge me, at least not for a while now. Not since I took over Massimo's seat as head of La Famiglia. But something about her voice draws me in, excites me.

She presents a challenge and I fucking love it.

"Who are you?" I ask, stepping further into the office.

She's unamused and marches over to my sister's desk to drop the creased papers messily in the center. Not that Gemma's space was organized, anyway. "Listen." She places a hand on either hip, giving me a keen expression. "What do you need, buddy? You're here to see Giuseppe or you're not. Pick one."

She doesn't falter. Doesn't blink. Just stands there waiting for my answer.

Her attitude only piques my interest. "Tell me your name." I feel a smile rise on my face and for once I cannot hide it. I step closer to her, slowly, as if she might bite. She might, the look on her face is vicious.

"Rhea." She spits, as if giving me her name is a painful venture. Like I'm beneath her. The accent she boasts differs from mine, or anyone in Providence really. It's thicker, has less of the Northeast quality than mine has. Seems more authentic.

"Well, Ray-uh," I repeat, sounding her name out the same way she pronounced it. "Where's my father?" I ask her. I'm closer to her now, practically in her face. She's calm, not shaking, her fingers are still as they wrap around her forearm. I've met men

17

more panicky in my presence than she is. She holds her own.

"Oh," she says, the shape of her mouth curving with the word. "You must be one of his sons." Her eyebrow raises as she assesses me. "Gian, right? Because I'm told Gio is the nicer one." She steps back, turning away from me, not waiting for a response. "He's in his office." She flings a hand toward the door of my father's office.

I chuckle.

Damn, that sass.

Chapter Two

RHEA

Gian fucking DelGado.

King of Providence.

His attitude grates at my fragile nerves. He's too full of himself, too confident. I want to knock him down a few pegs. Men like him are used to getting what they want, and for once, I want him to walk away a loser.

"Hey." He follows me into my office, pulling on my arm to spin me around.

I lower my gaze to his hand that's wrapped around my forearm, before slowly bringing my attention back up to his eyes.

"Easy, killer." He chuckles, letting me go.

I turn my back to him again, trying my best to ignore the

man who stalked into my office like he owns the place. His eyes wander the room, assessing its bare state. The cream walls lack any artwork, the surface of my walnut desk is empty except for my laptop and a few papers. I have no pictures and no personal items. I can see the gears spinning in his mind. He's wondering why I lack any form of personality.

I don't, for the record.

I just have no intentions of making this office into my home.

Men like him believe the world revolves around them and everyone should bow down.

I don't give out loyalty like lollipops. My respect has to be earned.

"Do you need something?" I ask again, smoothing out my skirt and sitting down at my desk.

He leans in from the spot across from me, placing each of his enormous hands on the surface and getting into my personal space again. "Why are you being such a bitch?" He asks, a small look of amusement lining his features.

My nostrils flare at his use of the word bitch. Women with any amount of backbone are called the slur. If we don't sit down and shut up, we're bitches. Don't spread our legs and call them daddy, we're prudes.

It's a loser's war.

"Why are you acting like an entitled boy?" I retort.

His lips curve back up, pleased to see me playing his game.

I exhale heavily and turn away from him. "Please leave my

office."

"When did this become your office?" he asks, his lips pressed into a thin line as he regards me.

That's right. I'm reminded that this office was being saved for him. His father had hopes that Gian would follow in his footsteps. It was no secret that Giuseppe wanted one of his boys to be like him. But he didn't, neither of them did. Instead, he rose up the ranks of the mafia so at thirty-one he could be Il Capo.

And to another mafia daughter, that would be an impressive accomplishment.

But not me.

"Giuseppe hired me not too long ago." I tell him, my arms still firmly placed across my chest.

"Gian, leave Rhea alone, please." Giuseppe finally appears in the doorway with a heavy sigh.

"Rhea," he repeats, the name finally clicking in his mind. "Ah," the realization strikes him. "Joe's girl."

I cringe. Being my father's daughter is not my proudest accomplishment. I went to law school after all. Still, in Providence, that's all I'm known for.

Joe Cabrera's daughter.

I huff, slapping my hands on my hips. Gian is grating on my last nerves. I have the urge to step out of my heels, take out my hoops, and fight him like I did the girls in high school who had the nerve to call me the whore's daughter.

Because the second thing I'm known for is being the mistress's daughter.

One nobody would have known about, a fact that wouldn't have bothered my father, if my mother wouldn't have died. She left me in the care of my biological father at ten years old. The father who never wanted me. He just didn't want to use a condom.

"Gian." Giuseppe repeats, an edge to his voice.

Gian holds eye contact and then winks, straightening himself out and following his father out of my office.

My blood is still simmering as I watch his ass strut out my door.

"Your brother sucks." I tell Gemma, as I enter her bedroom, a bottle of red wine in my grip.

"Which one?" she asks, simultaneously holding up a t-shirt. She looks it over skeptically before tossing it in the black garbage bag instead of the box she's packing.

"Gian." I tell her. "You've been packing for about four weeks." I add, her move to Liam's house has been elongated by more than a month at this point.

She gives me a pointed look, holding up her fingers to tick off her bullet points. "Gian is an asshole," she says, one finger up. "And it's been three weeks, not four. Don't be dramatic." She slaps the hand down, hitting her thigh with a clap.

Tension sits between the members of the DelGado family since the newly founded Italian-Irish friendship, and at the center is Gemma. She won't admit it to me, but I think she's dragging her feet on leaving her father behind alone in this big house. Next, she'll be telling him she's leaving the law office and everything that keeps them close in proximity will cease to exist.

Her wedding day took place in the courthouse with just her father, brothers, and Liam's mother. She claims she had no desire to have a big drawn out wedding, but I can see a hint of sadness in her eyes when she speaks of it. I don't believe it's Giuseppe that disapproves of her relationship, more likely it's her prick of an older brother.

Unlike me, she has a good relationship with her father. Leaving him behind is hurting her, so I shut my mouth even though I know she's been packing the same box for *four* weeks. Instead, I twist off the cap of the wine bottle.

"Twist off?" Gemma shoots me a look as I remove the cap, its lack of a cork shouts *cheap.*

"I have an allowance." I tell her, pouring the contents of the bottle into two glasses I snagged from downstairs.

She snorts a laugh, taking the newly filled glass from me. "Why did Joe give you an allowance at twenty-five?"

"Good question." I shrug between sips of the potent liquid. "Another way to control me, I'd assume."

Controlling me is my father's favorite hobby. I'm the unwanted child, the daughter he didn't need or desire. He knew of me, sure, for those first ten blissful years he wanted nothing to do with me.

Then my mom got sick, and it wasn't long after that she passed away, leaving me in his care since she had placed his name on the birth certificate. I'm not the daughter he hoped for, that's a fact he's made abundantly clear.

In his view, my mother, while a good mistress, filled my head with nonsense. Everything I say elicits a groan from him and causes him to look to the sky and curse the woman.

My brother, on the other hand, is a saint in his eyes. Christopher, a whopping ten months older than me, can do no wrong. He stops by the house daily, consulting my father and visiting his mother. He's following closely in my father's footsteps, already running his own construction gambit, an extension of my father's.

The only difference between my father and Christopher is my affection. While I can't stand to be in the same room as my father, my brother is my best friend.

It's funny to me that the one in my house who gave me life is the one I hate the most. Elena, my stepmother, would say it's because we're too much alike. But I can't find a single similarity with my father.

Ringing pierces our ears, and I groan. I have a special ringtone set for my father, the man cannot handle being ignored, and a stipulation of him paying for law school was for me to "behave." Behave is a loose term, one that he manipulates to get me to fit his mold.

To Gemma's credit, she gives me space as I answer the call, switching into my friendly voice and pretending that I don't hate the man on the other end of the phone.

"I want you to come home now." He doesn't give me a hello

or ask how my day was, simply speaks his request with no room for negotiation.

"I'm at Gemma's."

"Then leave."

Seven years of higher education spoiled me. Sure, I still had to come home for holidays and comply with all his wild requests, but there was freedom at my fingertips. An apartment where he wasn't, space away from him. I've grown addicted to that freedom, in love with who I am away from him.

But he has me trapped, as I'm sure he intended. I'm free of student loans, the only blessing really, but I've got no money to my name. My father controls the bank account where Giuseppe deposits my paychecks. Every aspect of my financial-being is under his thumb.

And without money, I have no escape.

So I suck in a breath and tell him I'll be home soon, even though every bone in my body is aching and I want to scream.

Christopher is sitting at the dining room table when I get home. Not a rare occurrence considering how much time he spends here. If I had my own apartment like him, no amount of money would bring me back to this house.

There's a glass of amber liquid resting between his palms, the sides sweating almost as much as he is.

"Sis," he smiles, but it doesn't reach his eyes. It's forced. And Christopher normally greets me with a bear hug, squeezing me tightly until I cry for him to release me, just like when we were kids.

Christopher watched a broken ten-year-old girl walk through his front door, one who wasn't wanted anywhere, and made it his mission to make her smile. Still, fifteen years later, he's claiming the role of my best friend.

"What?" I ask, dropping my bag in the foyer, something Elena will surely scold me for. "What's going on?" I can see through his lackluster attitude that something is wrong.

Dark eyes avoid mine as he runs a hand through his hair, a slight hissing noise leaving his mouth. "Don't overreact." He tells me, lifting his hands as if guarding himself from me.

Instantly, I'm defensive.

Christopher knows me better than anyone. No friend or acquaintance has broken past all my shields the way Christopher has. Hell, he was there when I built most of them, watching the walls I constructed brick by brick.

My father comes out of the kitchen before Christopher can say anymore. He's dressed for a business meeting in black slacks and a button down. He yanks a few of the buttons open and the belt around his waist sags, recently loosened. While he was probably an attractive man at one point, I can't help but to find my father sloth-like now. His gut, a bit too large, his head too bald. He looks like a man who indulges too much. Too much food, booze, cigars.

With a huff, he sits down at the head of the table and gestures for me to take the seat to his right. Wordlessly, I do. The atmosphere in the room is chilling. Goose bumps rise on my flesh while I wait for him to say whatever it is he demanded me home for. By the feel of things, it can't be good.

"Listen," he says, clasping his hands together on the table in front of him. In the kitchen I can hear the fan over the stove, something boiling, and the rhythmic sound of Elena stirring sauce. My pulse picks up the longer it takes for him to spit it out, I can't stand the anticipation.

"I spoke with Russ Valentino in Buffalo, his son Ronan is interested in marrying you. It would be an excellent match."

Clarity leaves me. The room is hazy, shrouded with clouds of red at the edge of my vision. I feel wobbly, like I might tip out of my chair if I don't grasp onto the table. I forget to breathe, air rushing from my lungs and not refilling. I'm not sure what else my father says, I'm still stuck on the first few words that left his lips in such a nonchalant manner, as if it wasn't my life he was discussing, but the local news.

Finally, I suck in a breath. Letting the oxygen fill my lungs as if for the first time and like a baby just entering the world, I want to scream.

"What?" The words leave my lips, deep and hoarse. "What are you saying?" I ask.

"I accepted. You're marrying the Valentino boy."

I feel my hands slap down on the dining room table, shaking the thing, before I even realize what I'm doing. Christopher mutters something at the other end, but I don't hear it, still overcome with the red haze that's blocking out everything except me and my father.

"No." I say.

He's looking at me the way you would a feral animal. As if I'm wild and untamed. I might bite if he shows his fear, so he stands, hovering over me. "You will marry this boy, Rhea Estella Cabrera. You will walk down the aisle and marry him." His voice rises, growling the last few words at me.

I stand too, meeting his eyes. They're brown, unlike my green ones. I like to imagine I got all my best features from my mother, but my anger, this came from him.

"No." I say. I'm shorter than him, so he still hovers over me. His fingers tense, gripping against the table while he tries to restrain himself from hitting me.

Because we both know hitting me doesn't work.

"Rhea." He repeats, this time angrier. He's about to lose his temper, letting it bubble until it explodes over the edge. When he gets like this, he's mean. He'll shout while he causes destruction, tossing lamps and books and anything within his reach.

Growing up, guessing how his anger would manifest was like a game for me. If I refuse to finish my dinner, will he break the plate? If I talk back, will he bruise my skin, blacken my eye?

So that's why Elena's in the kitchen, I realize, she's distracting herself so she doesn't have to take part in the argument. She's distant for the same reason Christopher is drinking. Neither of them agree, but neither will do anything to stop it.

And after fifteen years of arguments between my father

and I, I understand why they don't step in. After all the yelling and screaming has quieted, he'll win, he always does. Still, his excellent track record hasn't stopped me from fighting.

What he says is law in this house, and no matter how much I beg and plead and cry, I never seem to sway him.

I slump down into my seat, letting defeat take over.

"Just one question," I say, my voice lower, disappointment coating my words. "What do you get from this arrangement?"

I don't believe for a second that my father has ever loved me. I think he loves Christopher, and that he loves the idea of Elena, but can't stand being stuck with one woman. But he will never convince me of his love for me.

And now, as he looks at me with such disdain, I know for certain that he's never cared for me. "A partnership." He says thickly. "A partnership that will make us all rich."

Money.

Because money is far more important than family.

"So it's done then?" I ask, defeat lacing my tone.

My father sighs, his hands hitting the thick rolls of his sides. "As soon as I get the approval from DelGado. It's as good as done."

As good as done. But not done.

Chapter Three

GIAN

I'm late when I finally arrive for Sunday dinner. Gemma has already loaded the plates full of pasta and garlic bread. Gio and my father sit at the table, both nursing a glass of amber liquid.

"Finally," my father calls when I come through, shutting the door behind me. Annie, Gio's wife, comes out from the living room, baby Gabi nestled into her chest and burp cloth over her shoulder. The new-mom weariness is clear in her eyes as she slides into the seat next to my brother.

To Gio's credit, he takes the baby from his wife, gently rocking her. I never thought I'd see my younger brother as a father, and definitely not before me, but it suits him. Annie brings out a different, better side of him. And Gabi is the light of his life.

"I'll help," I tell Gemma, eyeing her carrying multiple plates into the dining room. I toss my suit jacket onto a chair and grab two plates from her.

"So," she says, "Rhea said you stopped by the office looking for me? She also said you're a dick." Gemma looks over at me with a smug smile. Lately, our conversations stem around how much I suck. Or how much she hates me. Once she even threw out that being in my presence makes her physically ill.

I understand where she's coming from. Getting shot made me slightly more sympathetic to her, not enough to agree with her life choices, but enough to know I don't want to lose my sister over them.

I chuckle, a sly smile lifting the corners of my mouth. Regardless of whether or not her anger is justified, she's still my little sister, and she's still a brat. Sitting the plates down in front of my brother and father, I ask, "She's the one in the second office?"

"Yep." Gemma says with a pop. Her eyes find mine, sharing a knowing glance. My father kept that office open for me, hoping one day I'd join him and practice law. Even though I'm not using it and never planning to, it still feels... bad that he's finally given up on me.

Or maybe it's because he knows running *La Famiglia* suits me better than his job would.

"Well, she was being a bitch, so..."

Annie gasps at my curse. "Gian!" she scolds. "Not in front of the baby!" Her eyes shoot down to the sleeping girl. Gabi isn't even a year old yet, still a pale blob of life with no actual emotions yet. I don't think she minds.

"She can't hear." I shrug, eliciting a laugh from my brother. Gio's been different since marrying Annie and having the baby. He parties less, no longer drinking away his days and sleeping in his office. All of his attention has shifted to the two girls in his life.

I run a hand over my chin as I settle in my seat. "Well, it's the truth."

"She's not a bitch," Gemma retorts, tossing a napkin over her lap with added dramatics. "She just isn't charmed by you."

"Or anyone?" I ask. A girl with that attitude probably hasn't seen a dick in a while. Maybe she's never been with a man who knows how to punish that sassy mouth of hers. Or occupy it. I could help her with that.

Gemma's face turns, a frown marking her features and her lips pressed thin. She's silencing herself from telling me to fuck off. She won't say it in my father's presence. She waits until he's gone to remind me how little she thinks of me.

The truth that she won't admit is she's directing all of her anger at me when she knows damn well that my father and Gio weren't raising any objections. She's still holding a grudge from the day I found her in a hotel room exposing herself for the Irishman and dragged her ass back to Providence. She's trying to hide her anger, trying to be civil, but it lingers there.

"Rhea's nice," my father says. "Single too."

I snort a laugh, putting a frown on my father's face. Giuseppe has been dropping hints about marriage for far too long. He would never force me to settle down, never arrange something. He respects our freedom to choose far too much, but my single status is grating on him. "No, Papa." I say with a smile. "I'm not marrying the girl, and *nice* is not the qualification I'm looking for."

"Well, she wouldn't marry you," Gemma scoffs. "She has far better taste than that." I can't help but to laugh at her comment. If I wanted her to, Rhea would walk down the aisle and meet me at the altar. My status in *La Famiglia* holds more weight than she could fight, plus her dirtbag of a father would jump at the chance to have his daughter closer to the throne.

"Regardless." My father dismisses our bickering with a wave of his hand, a silent order that he's older than us and he wants us to listen. It's funny, even as an adult my mouth snaps shut and turns to him. He's always had my respect like that. "You need to marry." He says to me.

A groan escapes my lips. He's been harping on this for weeks. I'm young and single and the men don't see me as a real leader. They want stability and nothing says stability like a family man. Should I swap out my BMW for a minivan while I'm at it?

Not to mention the Feds. As a single man, I'm a gangster. A bully taking hard earned money off the streets. A husband and a father, though? He's just supporting his family.

As much as I hate to admit it, getting married would help my image.

The problem is, I don't want to marry. I don't want to be strapped down with a cinder block tied around my ankles. And it has nothing to do with sex. My job is dangerous; there's a chance one night I might not walk back through the front door. Why bring someone else into that when they didn't ask for it?

My heart rate picks up thinking about my mother. Images of her lifeless body dance through my head. Bullets pierced her heart, leaving her bloody and dead. Simply because her killers thought it was my father in the car. Why should I put a wife or a child at risk because of my choices? It doesn't sit well with me. So instead, I keep everything brief. No long-term relationships. No attachments. That way, they never get hurt and neither do I.

"They'll never see you as a boss if you don't," my father says, jabbing his red tinted fork at me.

I know he's right. But it's not like I even have someone to propose to.

I shake my head. "Sure, Pa," I say. "I'll get right on that."

Gio gives me a knowing look.

I will not be getting right on that.

"Boss?" Rapheal pokes his head into my office, his knuckles knocking twice on the frame of my door. He looks at me hesitantly. The man has worked for me less than a year, and for as big and muscular as he is, I still see him flinch in my presence. He's only ten years younger than me, the son of another made man and a recent addition to my crew.

"What?" I ask, lifting my gaze from the computer I've been staring at for the past two hours. Trying to do work for my legitimate businesses while my office is a revolving door for men who are a part of my other businesses.

I've worked for years to get to this position, the fucking top of the pyramid, and it's draining. Nonstop problems presented on silver platters with no solutions. Sometimes I feel like I'm surrounded by the cast of Dumb and Dumber.

I run a hand through my hair, irritated by the constant interruptions before lifting my gaze to meet a nervous Rafi. "What?" I ask again.

"It's the Cabrera girl. She's here, wants to see ya, boss."

Joe Cabrera. The Capo who gives me the most headaches. His daughter… ah, the sassy one from my father's office.

I lean back in my chair, interlacing my fingers behind my head. "Let her in."

Unlike my brother, who keeps a snazzy-looking office in one of our clubs, I like to work out of the pizza shop. The shop is the first business I ever took over, a small family style place with an old Italian cook who speaks little English. The smell of grease from the cheese constantly assaults my senses.

Expensive heels tap against the floor as Rhea enters my office. She looks around the space, taking inventory before her emerald eyes finally settle on me.

"Sit," I gesture to the seat across from my desk.

She sinks into the chair, clutching her designer purse to her chest. She's stunning, just like she was when I met her in my father's law office. Her dark hair sits in unruly curls, falling down her back. She's wearing a pair of slim fitting black pants with a tan cardigan and matching high heels. The outfit looks expensive and fashionable.

Her foot taps a quick rhythm as she looks at me cautiously. She's more nervous than she was when I met her days ago. Then she was aloof, annoyed by my presence. Now she has a mixture of disgust when she looks at me and something else... need.

What she needs? I don't know, but I can practically see it pooling in those sparkling green eyes of hers.

"What is it?" I ask.

Swallowing deeply, she meets my eyes when she speaks. "My father is going to ask you for permission to arrange my marriage to the son of a Capo from Buffalo." She tells me, avoiding any small talk, which I appreciate.

"So?" I ask. She fidgets with her hands, trying to restrain herself from saying anything mean, I can't practically see it rising off of her. "Why are you telling me this?" I ask, annoyance tinging my tone.

She takes a deep inhale, steeling her spine and calming her nerves. "I'd like you to tell him no."

"And why would I do that?"

"Because arranged marriages are silly and outdated," She spits. The fire is slowly coming back to her, even though I can see that she's attempting to restrain herself. I kind of want to see what she looks like when she lets go, let the fire rage and burn everything around her. I bet she's stunning when she's free from the restraints.

"That's why you're in my office? To tell me it's silly of your father wanting to arrange your marriage?" I lean forward, placing my elbows on my desk.

Rhea's lips are pressed thin, her knuckles white and wrapped tightly around the handles of her purse. Whatever she came here to ask me, she's not happy about it. Clearly the idea of needing my help physically pains her.

"Why?" I ask again.

"Because I don't want to." The words rush from her mouth with a hiss, giving me the truth.

"Ah," I lean back in my chair, admiring her honesty and her balls for coming into my office and asking me to deny her father. If he knew she was here she'd have hell to pay.

"I'm not normally one to get involved in domestic disputes." I give her a small smile. It's not quite a lie, I rarely get involved with how my men run their familie. As long as they're not making headlines for beating their wives, they can do whatever they want.

Those green eyes glare at me, the anger rising to her features. "I thought you were a family man? Would you let your sister have an arranged marriage?" She looks cocky after asking, as if it would pull on my heartstrings.

"If it got her away from that fucking Irishman, I would arrange her marriage in a second." I smile as the words leave my lips. That statement is genuine. I would happily see Gemma through a divorce if it meant getting away from Liam. While I can't deny that having the Irish war behind us has been good, I still don't like the guy.

Rhea huffs loudly and the sight of her irritation amuses me. She puffs out her chest and avoids my gaze. I can see the gears turning in her head as she tries to assemble a comeback.

After a moment she slumps her shoulder and turns her face back to mine, her eyes glassy and pleading. "Please, Gian. I'm asking you to please tell him no."

Her emerald eyes are pleading with me.

"Why?" I ask. "Why are you so adamant not to marry?" If she's going to ask me for a favor, she's going to pay by sharing all her secrets.

"I-" She closes her eyes, composing herself before she continues. "I'm studying for the bar and I'd like to be a lawyer and that would intimidate most men in our circle. I don't want to give up my dreams to be a housewife."

When she looks at me, I see her sincerity. Her fear in admitting those words to me sits plain as day on her face. In our world, secrets are used against you and it's clear she knows that by the frown marking her pretty face. She risked a lot by coming here, by begging me to help her. I could easily call Joe as soon as she leaves. I could tell her to leave and give her pending marriage my blessing.

If she's smart, she realizes all of this. And still she sits across from me, asking for my help.

"I'll see what I can do," I tell her, waving my hand to dismiss her.

She stands, turning for the door, readying herself to leave. "Thank you," she tells me over her shoulder and then she's out the door.

"Rafi," I call and almost immediately he is in my doorway. "Set up dinner with Joe Cabrera, please. His house preferably. And I want everything you can get on his daughter, Rhea. Discreetly please."

With a nod, Rafi leaves me.

But the thoughts of Rhea Cabrera surging through my head don't.

Chapter Four

RHEA

Elena is setting the table when I get home from work. I can practically feel the anxiety wafting off of her as she twists napkins into perfect rolls of fabric and sets them over her good dishes.

"What's going on?" I ask, shrugging off my coat and hanging it by the door. Elena only uses the nice dishes when we have company or when her parents come. Otherwise, they're tucked away in the china cabinet and dusted weekly. I've never understood the appeal of having dishes that we never use. Why not enjoy your possessions rather than admire them from afar?

"Put that away," Elena scolds, wagging a rolled napkin at me. "And we're having guests for dinner."

I grab the coat I just took off, tucking it under my arm. "Who?" It's not unusual for Elena to have friends over for dinner or other couples, normally other mafia wives, but she never pulls out the good dishes for them.

Elena swivels, running a hand through her dyed blonde hair. "The DelGados are coming over tonight."

My heart stops for a minute, flashes of my conversation with Gian just this morning run through my brain. "Why?" I blurt.

Elena shrugs, releasing a long breath. "I don't know, but your father plans to ask him about the marriage. Gian's his boss now, so this is an important dinner for him."

Dread courses through my veins. My father plans on asking Gian tonight at a dinner with my entire family after I asked him to deny this marriage this morning. It was stupid to ask him. I barely know him and for all I know he could plan to rat me out to my father as we all cut into our chicken. *Oh, by the way Joe, your daughter went behind your back and asked me to say no to the question you haven't even asked me yet.*

I run a hand through my curls and exhale a ragged breath. This has the possibility to go terrible for me.

"Don't mess up your hair," Elena scolds. "And can you wear something nicer?" My stepmother is normally not a mean woman, but when she gets stressed, she becomes overly sensitive about everything. Her nit picking becomes intense, suddenly she can point out a wrinkle from a mile away.

"Yes." I sigh. "I'll change. Do you need help in the kitchen?" I ask, receiving a grateful look from Elena.

"Please," she answers.

"I'll be down in a minute." I tell her, heading up the stairs to my bedroom. Christopher is at the top of the landing, leaning against the doorframe to my bedroom. "What are you doing here?" I ask, pushing past him and into my bedroom. Twenty-five and still living at home. It feels wrong, but there's no way in hell my father would approve of me living on my own.

"I'm joining you for dinner tonight."

"Great, so you can witness my humiliation first hand?"

He gives me a cheeky smile. "You're being dramatic, Sis." He plops himself onto my bed, a sure way to wrinkle his dress pants and piss his mother off.

"You get to say that because this will never happen to you." I move to my closet, sifting through the arrangement of dresses. The one good thing about living with Elena and my father is Elena still takes me shopping. My closet is filled with clothes, and designer brands that I wouldn't be able to buy without her credit card.

I pull out a black short-sleeved silk dress with a flowing midi skirt. The color seems appropriate for the occasion, the death of my freedom. I shut the closet door to change while Christopher sits on my bed.

"It's going to be fine," he tells me as I emerge from the closet.

"Easy for you to say," I tell him, fluffing my curls in the mirror. "You'll never have a decision like this made for you. You'll always get a choice in the matter, Chris." I spin around to face him. "Can you even imagine what it's like to be told your opinion doesn't matter? That I don't even get a say in my own marriage?"

Christopher rubs a hand over his jawline. It's clear that he expected this conversation to go differently. "Just give it a chance, Rhe," he says, a pathetic pleading tone to his voice. He's always been so soft and gentle with me. So different from my father, I can't imagine him to be a gangster. But that's a good thing. Chris has a good heart, inherited from Elena and definitely not our father.

I swipe a fresh coat of red lipstick over my lips before heading back down to the kitchen to help Elena. She has yet to change, still wearing a pair of leggings and a baggy t-shirt and stirring a pot of sauce, the steam rising to heat her cheeks.

"Elena," I grab the spoon from her. "I got this."

The one thing Elena and I have always been able to bond over is cooking. I was silent when they brought me into this house. I had never met my father, instead spending a blissful ten years with just my mother, so when he brought me to his home where he had a wife and a son, I had no desire to be a part of this family. And he made no effort to make me feel otherwise. If it wouldn't have looked so bad for him, he probably would have shoved me into foster care.

Elena, however, was patient and kind. When I didn't talk, she showed endless patience and when she found out I liked to be in the kitchen, she spent hours teaching me how to roll pasta dough and make spaghetti. We baked cookies and breads, constantly

44

learning new recipes. When we weren't in the kitchen, we sat in front of the TV watching the Food Network. When I finally spoke again, it was to her first.

She gives me a thankful look, a pat on the shoulder and rushes upstairs to her bedroom to change. My father walks into the kitchen as soon as she exits, letting his eyes slide up and down my body, looking over the heels on my feet and the fabric covering me with a critical eye. I'm never quite enough for him and normally he's keen to brush me off, but tonight I play a part in his plan.

I assume I must look fine when he says nothing, instead passing by me and pulling out a bottle of beer from the fridge.

When he walks back by me he utters only a few words, "Behave tonight, girl."

Gian looks even better than this morning when he enters our house, slipping a black coat off and handing it to Elena with a charming smile. I hate myself for admiring his good looks, but they're hard to ignore, which I'm sure is why he's so goddamn cocky.

He looks fresh with slicked back dark hair and a clean-shaven face. Behind him his father and brother enter, no Gemma in sight. My chest aches. Gemma would definitely be my saving grace. She's more like me than Elena. Not the pristine mafia princess, she speaks her mind, and with her marriage to Liam O'Connor she's breaking all the norms in our families.

"Rhea," Gian grins, tipping his head to me. "Nice to see you again."

My father shoots me a look, daggers flying from his eyes. "You two have met?" He looks concerned at the thought of me meeting his new boss, as if I'm such a poor representation of him.

I smile sweetly. "At Giuseppe's office." I say. "Gian stopped by yesterday." I let myself glance at Gian for only a second. His expression has only gotten more smug as he watches me act innocently.

The dynamic has completely shifted from when he walked into the office the other day. He has all the power now that I've asked him for help. Betrayal is an option that sits on the table. With a few words, he could shatter me.

Or he can help me. Get me out of the forced arrangement. It would piss my father off, but it would prevent me from being at the mercy of another man. A man possibly worse than my father.

"Sit," Elena says, leading the three men into the dining room. My father sits at the head of the table. Elena and Christopher take the two seats next to him and Gian takes the seat at the other end of the table, the rest of us filtering in between them. Somehow, I end up sitting next to the man with his brother directly across from me.

My father says a quick prayer before we begin eating. I bring my fingers to the cross that sits at the base of my throat. The gold charm was the one my mother wore her entire life. It's one of the few things I have left from her. My father was keen to erase all memories of her as quickly as possible, not wanting the weight of his affair to be present in this household. My old furniture, clothing, toys—he tossed it all in the trash. I gripped the gold cross in my palm as I watched him deconstruct my life.

Now I twist the pendant in my fingers, anchoring myself as I listen to the godless man pray.

When he finishes, we all open our eyes, mine glancing over at Gian who studies the charm gripped in my fingers. I drop it immediately, refusing to let him know what it means to me.

I've learned in this life that your secrets need to stay that-secret. These men, these people, will use anything they can against you and I refuse to give them any leverage over me. Well, anymore than they already have.

Dinner passes by in a flurry of conversation. My sweaty palms can barely grip my fork, so I spend most of the time pushing food around on my plate instead of eating it. It all tastes like ash in my mouth, anyway. I'm too anxious to eat, too on edge to taste anything.

"So," Gian says, after Elena and I have cleaned up and served coffee and cheesecake. "You had something you wanted to talk about?" He looks at my father.

"Yes," Joe answers, patting the seam of his lips with his cloth napkin. "My daughter, Rhea," he gestures to me with his fork. "She's twenty-five now, way past time for her to be married, I think."

A scoff escapes my lips at his words. In no world is twenty-five old. It's outdated to think I need to be married by now. My father shoots me a look, a silent warning to be quiet.

"I have been speaking to the Valentinos in Buffalo. He has a son interested in Rhea. We've been talking business and he has a supplier in Buffalo I think would be beneficial to our organization. He can up his order to provide more for us at a discounted rate. I think it's a good deal." He says.

"In exchange for marrying Rhea?" Gian asks, tilting his head ever so slightly.

"Yes."

My father and Gian stare at each other for a moment. It feels like forever before Gian speaks again.

"I have a counteroffer," he says. "I'll marry Rhea."

I think my heart stops beating. There's an aching in my chest. I don't hear what else Gian says, what he gives to sweeten the deal. This was worse than the possibilities that filtered through my head. I thought he would either rat me out or help me. Never did the possibility that he would claim me as his own enter my head.

"No," I shout out before I can even fully comprehend what I'm saying.

All heads turn to me. Panic courses through my body, my heart suddenly beating way too fast. "No," I repeat. "I don't want to marry anyone."

"Rhea," My father scolds.

"No." Gian waves a hand in a silencing gesture. "She can speak."

My father looks like he's about to explode, all the blood rushing to his head and threatening to combust.

Gian stands from his chair, wiping invisible dust from his slacks. He walks over to me, still standing in the doorway between the kitchen and dining room, a pot of coffee in my hands. Gian takes the pot, walking over to the table and setting it down gently. The eyes of our five family members watch our every move.

"Can I have a second with your daughter, Joe?" Gian asks. "Alone?"

With my father's blessing, Gian leads me into the kitchen, closing the door behind us and giving us the semblance of privacy. His fingers grip around my waist to spin me quickly, pressing me against the counter.

"Rhea," he whispers, a smug smile still lingering on his cheeks. "What are you doing?"

"This wasn't what I asked for!" I spit back, trying my best to keep my voice low. "You asked me to say no to your pending marriage and I did." He has a cocky look on his face that makes my blood boil.

He knows damn well what I asked for and he twisted this situation, took advantage of my vulnerable state and used it against me. I practically growl in his face.

"No," I sneer. "I don't want to marry anyone."

He tsks at me, his tongue hitting the roof of his mouth as he presses his hips into me, pushing me against the counter. His warm breath skates across the sensitive skin on my neck as he leans in. "You asked for my help and I'm helping you. You should be more grateful." The words hit my ear in a whispered tone. I can smell the whiskey and cedarwood scent of him; it infiltrates my senses, an attack on my nose. He's too close, demolishing my personal space and taking me hostage.

My palms hit his chest in a futile attempt to push him off of me. "Fuck you," I sneer. His chest is a hard wall of muscle, unmoved by my shoves.

"Listen to me," he says, gripping my wrists into his hands to stop my attack. "We both have something to gain from this situation. You don't want to marry that prick in Buffalo? Done. You want to take the bar and not be a housewife. Done. I won't stop you from doing any of that. All I want is a pretty woman, which you are, bella. As long as you join me when I need you, wear a pretty little dress like this." His eyes drift down to my dress. "I'll be a happy man. I won't ask a ton from you, you can do whatever the fuck you want. And it will get you out of this house. Your father's a dick, by the way." He releases my hands after his speech and steps back. "It's your choice, *cara*," he adds. "But you have to make it now."

His speech is compelling. The idea that I can get out of my father's thumb is the most enticing of all the things Gian promised. Adding in that I continue to study for the bar, maybe start my own practice. He practically offered me all my dreams. The only problem is I have to marry him.

"What's it gonna be?" he asks.

I could do worse for a husband. At least Gian is attractive.

"I can practice law?" I ask skeptically.

"Of course."

"And I won't have to host parties like this?" I gesture to the dining room.

Gian laughs. "We might have to host some parties, but we can get them catered or something. I'll make it easy on you."

He looks cute when he smiles but he's still an asshole. This changes nothing, even if he's right. It's a better offer than anything else I'll get.

"Fine," I say. "Consider yourself engaged."

Chapter Five

GIAN

There's a look of smug satisfaction on Joe Cabrera's face when we agree on the new engagement. He's thrilled that his daughter will marry me and even happier that it puts him in a position of power. For the first time, he might be proud of his bastard child.

The file Rafi dropped off on my desk this afternoon proved interesting. I expected a few details. The daughters of my men tend to be boring. Private school kids, decent grades, okay colleges. They're not exceptional, but not bad by any means. Sadly, they're seen as currency, a daughter in exchange for a lucrative business deal.

But Rhea's file… hers is a little out of the ordinary.

The daughter of first and second generation Italian immigrants. Isabella D'Amelio migrated from Florence twenty-five years ago with nothing but the clothes on her back. Her reason for fleeing her home country was left out of the file. I'm assuming it went unknown. Pictures of Isabella showed a bright eyed and bushy tailed twenty-something woman. Strikingly beautiful with wild dark curls and bright green eyes, the spitting image of Rhea.

Quickly, after her arrival to Providence, she became pregnant. Somehow she had become a mistress to Joe, the man newly married with a child on the way. The timing between the births of his two children puts Rhea's conception around the time Christopher was only a few weeks old. The thought of him cheating while Elena was home with a newborn makes my blood boil, but his indiscretions from twenty-five years ago aren't mine to judge.

After realizing that Joe had no intentions of marrying her, Isabella was left to raise her baby on her own.

Then she got sick. Aggressive breast cancer that went untreated for far too long. Isabella was uninsured and poor as fuck, so treatment was off the menu. When the cancer was finally discovered, she only had a few months of life left to live.

At ten years old, Rhea was thrust into the arms of a father she had never met.

I cringed reading that. Imagining a small child being thrown into a family she never knew existed. Not to mention what it must have been like for Elena and Christopher to suddenly have another child in the house, a constant reminder of his indiscretions.

Joe is an asshole, something I've known since I met him as a child.

How much of an asshole I was just finding out.

Rhea is quiet for the rest of dessert, a first for her. I'm assuming she's seeing herself as an object, being passed off to her new owner and with her history I can understand that. She only speaks when I ask her to plan the engagement party for the following weekend.

"No," she says, arms crossed over her chest. "I don't do parties."

I shoot her a look, hoping it conveys my message of *you don't have a fucking choice.* "It's an engagement party," I say. "We have to announce the damn engagement." Next to me, Gio chuckles, bringing a glass of cognac to his lips.

"I can plan it," Elena interrupts, possibly the first time I've ever heard the woman speak. She's different from her stepdaughter. If you didn't know it, you wouldn't think this is the woman who raised Rhea for over half her life. Elena is polite and quiet, the perfect mafia wife. Rhea is the exact opposite of her. Her face broadcasts her thoughts, displaying them in the form of flared nostrils and narrowed eyes. Any comment that leaves those red painted lips is snarky and rude.

She's a bitch.

But she's damn gorgeous.

If I wanted an actual wife, I can't say that Rhea Cabrera would be my first pick. She's too mouthy, too opinionated. But I don't want an actual marriage. I just need the appearance of one to solidify my place in La Famiglia, and Rhea fits the bill perfectly.

Full-blooded Italian with good looks. Other men will weep at her high heel clad feet.

It doesn't hurt that she is a well-bred Italian woman. Her clothes boast designer labels, the soles of her shoes a bright red. The handbag she carried into my office earlier today had the Cartier logo stitched to the front. And then there are her looks, the olive complexion, dark hair, and slim frame. The girl is absolutely perfect.

Nobody needs to know that this whole thing is a sham.

"We should pick a date," Joe says. I glance over at Rhea's face to see her lips pressed thin. She still doesn't like this, and maybe I'm an asshole for not talking to her first and instead backing her into a corner, but at the end of the day we would have arrived at the same place. Our pending marriage.

Because she knows as well as I do that this is the only way to keep her father off her back and her dreams intact.

"Soon," I say.

Rhea whips her head to me, her hair flying behind her back while those green eyes shoot daggers at me. "What?"

"Soon," I repeat. "As soon as possible." My eyes meet hers in a standoff, a silent war between the two of us. She's already not fully on board with the wedding. If I gave her the option, she would drag her feet as long as possible, but I have a business to run and La Famiglia doesn't have time to wait around on a spoiled child.

"Gi-"

"Elena," I cut Rhea off, "Do you want to plan a wedding too? Since my bride has an aversion to party planning?" Gio snorts a laugh at my comment. Rhea's face has turned vicious, practically snarling in my direction.

"Sure," Elena says, giving me a polite smile. "Any requests for dates?" she asks.

"As soon as possible," I answer again, bringing my glass of cognac to my lips and keeping my eyes trained on my new fiancée. I won't say I'm a decent man. Nowhere near good. However, I'd like to think I'm a better man than the asshole that sits at the other end of the table and calls himself a father.

At least with me, Rhea knows what she's getting herself into.

She huffs loudly and slumps back into her seat. She's pissy and I won't force her to suppress her feelings. She's allowed to be angry.

But she agreed to this.

"The mayor is on TV." Shelly, the new server Sal hired at the pizza shop, grabs the remote from the counter and turns up the volume on the mounted flat screen. She's not the brightest girl Sal's hired, but I keep my mouth shut. Sal takes care of his own business with little intervention from me and if Shelly isn't smart enough to keep her mouth shut, Sal will cut her loose. One of the many reasons I love the man.

Our city's mayor of two years, a slim balding man, steps up to the podium on the TV with a grim face and a few papers clutched in his grip. He inhales deeply as he straightens the paper and looks at the crowd gathered on the steps of city hall.

He has the look of a man that's about to do something very, very stupid.

"I've always believed that public service was my fate. I belong here to serve the public, the great people of Providence…" His speech makes me want to put a bullet in my skull. All politicians talk the same talk. They claim they do this job to serve the people, the great people of their cities. But it's all garbage. They do this for themselves, for the clout that comes with being an elected official. Every move they make is to stay in power, not to better the lives of the people who elected them. Hell, they would burn their cities to the ground if it meant more power.

I've never believed in fate.

I never once humored the idea of a bigger, divine purpose. The phrase, 'everything happens for a reason' grates on my soul, fraying my nerves. I don't believe in reasons, don't believe there is something watching over me and guiding me in the right direction.

Everything I have, I made with my two bare hands. I clawed my way through the dark underbelly. Bathed in the blood of those who thought to spite me. I killed for my chance at the throne, watched my friends leave this world in front of my eyes. Everything I've ever done has my fingerprints etched on it. I take credit for my failures, my victories.

No one ever led me here, no one ever mapped it out in the big plan and wrote my name here.

I did this.

I worked my ass off to earn the moniker King of Providence and I won't let this city be taken from me.

Not by the Irish.

Not by some stupid elected official.

And surely not by the fucking FBI.

"Unfortunately," he continues blabbing on the TV. "Our great city has become overrun with crime. The Mafia has made their bed here. They eat at our restaurants, shop in our stores. They have embedded themselves in our lives and it's time for us to say enough."

I can't help the laugh that escapes my lips at his pretty speech. Our beloved Providence mayor has decided he's too good for us now. Too good for the group of men that ensured him his spot in city hall.

Two years ago, when Mayor Anderson was running for office, he wasn't too good for us. He came to me on his knees, asking for votes, for protection, and I granted his every wish. I made him mayor of Providence, embedded a man in his security detail that could eliminate any threat. I gave him power.

And all he had to do in return was keep attention off my organization, let us run in fucking peace.

And the dick can't even do that right.

Stupid fucking move.

I slip my cell phone from my pocket and dial my brother's

number. "Gio, I want to know where Jimmy is? Seems our good friend in city hall no longer requires his service."

"On it."

Gio ends the call with a click while I continue to watch Anderson's speech. There's no substance beneath his pretty words. He says, 'we have to stop the mafia' but doesn't lay out how. He paints us as monsters, me the worst of them all.

And maybe I am a monster.

Maybe I'm the thing that goes bump in the night.

But you can't ask a monster for protection and then turn your back on him, that's not how this game works. And contrary to the bullshit that fairy tales feed you, the monsters always win.

Sal slides two slices of hot pizza on the table in front of me, the slices dripping with grease and melted cheese. I barely have one lifted to my lips before the chair across from me is scraped over the checkered floor and a body sits down.

The man who joins me has a wide grin directed at me. He leans his arms onto the square table and lets the sleeves of his trench coat stick to the red and white checkered cloth. "Gian DelGado," he growls.

I'm repulsed by his voice, the sheer cockiness of it makes me want to reach across the table and wrap my fingers around his throat. But I have to remain civil, I can't choke an FBI agent after all.

The asshole in front of me has a balding head with thin as hell hair and an ugly mug. I grimace at his presence. Special Agent

Aaron Baldwin, of the Providence field office, is the bane of my existence.

I lift my napkin, wiping the remnants of grease from my face before greeting him. "Aaron, horrible to see you again," I snide.

He likes to visit me here. I think it's because he secretly likes the food, even if he knows every purchase is money in my pocket.

"Same to you," he retorts, a sleazy smile rising on his face.

"So, you the new boss?" he asks.

Ah, putting two and two together. Aaron has been following me even before I took over Massimo's seat as the boss of La Famiglia. He's had his eye on me the past few years, waiting for me to make a mistake so he could take me down.

I don't make mistakes.

"Not sure what you mean," I answer, waving my hand to flag down Rafi. I've been running La Famiglia for over two years now. When Massimo died, there were only a few men that didn't respect me the way I required. Some are like that. The older generation are used to the way Massimo ran the business. It didn't matter though, because I was calling the shots regardless.

My man gives Aaron a small nod before looking at me, just barely polite. "Get our friend here a cup of coffee," I instruct him.

Aaron leans back into his seat, eyeing me as Rafi goes to the pot behind the counter, pouring a mug and bringing it back over to the table, slapping it down before the FBI agent and leaving without a word.

"Your friend," he nods his head to the TV where the mayor

is still giving his bullshit anti-crime speech. "Had a lot of very interesting things to say." He grins happily.

"Hmm." I take a sip of my own drink, letting the water wash down my throat slowly, keeping the agent waiting. "I've only met the man once, as I'm sure you know, so I don't know what you think is so interesting, but I'd be happy to hear." I match his grin as I set my glass back down on the table.

The man frowns, probably hoping to catch me off guard or rile me up. "You're not perfect," Aaron tells me. "You'll slip up soon and when you do, I'll be there." He grins, showing off his crooked, yellowed teeth as he reaches forward, lifting the mug and taking a gulp of coffee. "How about a to-go cup?" he asks, raising the ceramic and looking over at Rafi.

I give my man a nod and he grabs a styrofoam cup from behind the counter for the agent. Aaron pours the remnants of his coffee into the cup, sealing it with the lid and giving me a nod. "Thanks for the joe," He says, that slimy grin still in place. He rises from his seat and whistles on his way out like the smug bastard that he is.

"What a prick," Rafi exhales.

"Get me gloves and my fingerprint kit," I instruct Rafi, his eyebrows rising, giving me a confused look. "He left us some fingerprints." I nod to the mug he left on the table.

Rafi matches my grin. "What are you gonna do with them, boss?" he asks.

I shrug. I don't know yet, but I'm not missing an opportunity to have something on the man.

Chapter Six

GIAN

Providence Mayor killed in mob attack.

Flames and flashing lights flicker across my TV screen. A smug satisfaction crawls over my skin. I'm smiling as the iron glides over my French cuffed shirt, pressing out the wrinkles that mar the ivory fabric. I don't normally take satisfaction in the death of other men. Men that have wives and daughters, men that have shared my dinner table. I don't relish in knowing that their children will shed tears over their caskets and attend therapy for years to grieve their death.

Except in this case.

Because I warned Mayor Anderson.

We had several discussions on what his role in our arrangement was. I presented several opportunities. And he took none.

And now he's dead.

There's no room for misinterpretation, especially not now when my legacy is at stake. Every man who enters a position of power, be it the IT manager at Staples or a CEO of a Fortune 500 company, has a short time frame to show what they're made of before anarchy begins. If you do it right, everything settles, money is made, and your men are happy.

If you do it wrong… blood paints the city red.

Unfortunately, the mayor of my beloved city was on the wrong side of history.

The TV screen flashes a new picture while the reporter drones on. *Former leader of the Providence Mafia, Massimo Maranzano, killed in what police call a revenge mission only two years ago.*

Before his fall, before all the shit that went down leading to his death, I had nothing but admiration for Maranzano, the former boss of *La Famiglia.* A sick admiration considering I knew his tricks well. Still, his ability to manipulate any situation fascinated me. Twisting it to his own desires.

To our community, the Italian Americans who grew up in Providence, calling Federal Hill their home, Maranzano was a neighborhood man. They knew who he was, what he did, but the mafia meant something different to them. It was a neighborhood of Sicilian immigrants who viewed the mob as protectors. A brotherhood that cherished their own. And Maranzano was the best of them.

The week of Thanksgiving he would buy a truck full of

turkeys, driving through Federal Hill and tossing them out like Oprah.

If you had a problem, he would find you a solution. Couldn't pay rent? He'd give you the money, an interest free loan. Someone stole from you? He'd send someone to get your property back. Connections like this, little favors, built this community. When he called on you, that's when you repaid. And you never refused the Don.

That was what this organization was supposed to be.

La Famiglia.

In the years after his son's death, he destroyed all of that, every ounce of good will he had created. Shattering the oath that held this *Famiglia* together and causing a fracture so large there was no covering it.

It's taken time, endless amounts of favors and plenty of spilled blood to stitch this family back together.

No one, not even an elected official, is going to step in my way.

I slide the newly pressed shirt up my arms, securing the ivory buttons and tucking the fabric into the waistband of my slacks. My dad always said the suit makes the man, something I think he told me to make sure I wasn't running around in jeans and a wrinkled t-shirt, a trend loved by my younger brother. I took the message to heart, constantly making sure my appearance was perfect. Suits fitted and pressed, hair trimmed, jaw clear. My image and my reputation are spotless.

A quick knock sounds on the door, followed by my father's voice. Giuseppe enters the room with both hands shoved in the pockets of his charcoal gray suit. His dark brown eyes roam over me, assessing my attire and finding not a thread out of place as usual.

His eyes flicker to the TV atop the dresser in my childhood bedroom. "Ah," he says. "That's what's delaying you then?"

He's not wrong. My mental victory lap had distracted me. I celebrated inside the walls of my mind knowing I had won this round. My hands rise to smooth the lapels of my jacket and glide down my arms to adjust my cufflinks.

"Maybe," I smirk as I assess myself in the mirror.

"Dirty hands," my father mutters. "You need to distance yourself."

I shake my head. "I'm distanced," I smile widely. "Rafi handled it. I never lifted a finger."

"Good." My father huffs.

"Is my bride here already?" I ask with a smile.

Elena and Gemma held the engagement party at my father's estate, citing that it was bigger and it would be nice to have a celebration here. There was a sour look on Gemma's face as she told me, likely because her own wedding was not drawn out like this one. It was a quick courthouse marriage. Vows, sign the paper, and go on your merry way.

I had a hell of time convincing our relatives that she wasn't pregnant.

She was marrying an outsider, a fate we all agreed to, but it didn't mean that we liked it. At least not me. And despite my efforts to mend the broken relationship with my sister, she had no intentions of forgiving me.

The look on her face when she heard of my pending marriage was pure shock. She asked what I was holding over Rhea to force her to marry me. It offended me that my baby sister thought so little of me, but she wasn't wrong.

"No," my father answers, "But she should be here soon."

My father, while confused as to why I chose this path, was nonetheless thrilled. After two kids falling for outsiders and nontraditional weddings, Giuseppe was over the moon to have a traditional marriage in the family. Traditionally, in the *La Famiglia* sense. A big catholic church wedding with a huge reception and way too many people.

Any child's wedding in *La Famiglia* is an event to show off to everyone else, to show how wealthy and powerful you are. My marriage to Rhea was also solidifying me in my place at the top of this pyramid, showing me as a stable family man and the boss.

My soon-to-be wife didn't reach out to me at all this week. Not a single question, complaint, nothing. I thought she'd have something, some little remark or reminder that I backed her into a corner, but my bride gave me the cold shoulder.

She struts into my house on the heels of her father and brother. Christopher tucks his hands into the pockets of his slacks and looks up at me cooly. Christopher could easily have been me. His father and mine were friends growing up, but somehow Giuseppe got closer to the boss and Joe didn't. So while I was at mafia summer camp, Chris was running errands for his dad.

Unlike his father, though, he gives me a nod of respect.

Joe Cabrera, on the other hand, doesn't nod or shake my hand. He goes to my father first, giving his old friend a clap on the back. "So," he says, "Elena did a good job planning this party?"

My gaze locks onto Rhea, watching the way she rolls her emerald eyes at her father's remark. Probably another way to put her down, point out her flaws.

Immediately, I want her alone. I hate being around these people. Her family is a miserable group with Joe at the helm.

"Rhea," I say, extending my hand to her, "Let me show you around."

Green orbs scrutinize me, scanning my body while her red lips are strained in a thin line.

She agrees without a sound, stepping forward with a nude heeled foot and following me further into the house. "My father's office is back this way," I tell her, not sure if I'm actually giving her a tour or just helping her escape from her father for a momentary reprieve.

She takes her hand from mine once we're away from her family and my father.

"You don't need to take care of me," she says, wiping the hand that was just intertwined with mine down her dress as if she can't stand my touch lingering on her skin.

I stroke a hand over my jaw, my thumb tugging onto my lip while I admire my fiancée.

She's got balls. And damn, do I love them.

"Is that so?" I watch her lips turn, appalled by my retort. She has gorgeous full lips when she's not pressing them together. A tight fitted white dress clings to her curves, beneath the sheer lace is a nude liner making the dress somehow both sexy and sweet.

Long dark curls brush over the peaks of her chest. The desire to reach forward and wrap the locks around my fist, using it as a rope to drag her toward me flashes in my head. I'd love to see what that pouty mouth could do while she's on her knees.

I shake the thoughts from my head. This isn't a love-filled marriage, it's a fucking arrangement.

And my bride is bitter about it. Annoyance drips from her stance. Her demeanour is cold, uninviting.

The only way this girl will ever let me in her bed is if I force her. I'm a lot of things, but I'm not that.

The house is nearly cleared out when Gemma comes to find me, bouncing on the tip of her toes as if she's a little girl with a secret, her tell that she's trying to be sweet to butter me up. Gemma is good at playing the game, she works her cards perfectly. Acts sweet and loyal when she wants something, it's how she has our dad and Gio wrapped around her finger. I wonder if the disconnect between us is that I see through her act.

"Gian," she says, her pouty lips turning into a soft smile.

She spent the entire night occupying my soon-to-be wife, attached to her hip.

I wanted to do something, wrap an arm around Rhea's waist, drag her over to me. But what purpose would that serve? It's clear between the two of us that this marriage has no substance. The whole arrangement is purely for selfish reasons for each of us. Still, her utter dismissal of me drags red to the edges of my vision.

Never in my thirty-three years have I ever felt the desire for someone's respect. But for some stupid reason, I want Rhea to respect me.

And not because her father raised her to value men above herself.

I lift my eyes to Gemma, waiting for her to spit out whatever it is that she wants.

"Rhea and I want to go get drinks." She bats her long eyelashes, another trick she uses to get her way.

My fiancée stands further back from us, near my father, as if she's completely aloof to the plan my sister has concocted. She lifts a hand, dragging it through her thick curls.

She's a gorgeous woman, I would never deny that.

"Sure," I mutter, only because we've been engaged for one week and I'd hate for her to feel trapped underneath my orders. And Gemma is still angry with me and if I say no, she's likely to throw a fit.

A smile grows on her olive cheeks. "Thank you," she says, shock showing through her features. She probably thought she would have to fight me. I flash a look to Rhea, studying her as she tries to appear uninvested.

This kinship between my bride and my sister has the possibility to turn out badly for me. But if I shut it down now, it will only give her something to hold against me.

"Nicolas and Andrew will go with you," I add before Gemma can skip off and share her victory.

A pout forms on her painted lips. "Why?" she asks. My little sister has a hatred for being protected, having enforcers safeguard her. She likes to leave them in her dust, racing her cherry red Lexus so they can't keep up with her. I run my thumb across my lower lip, wondering if I need to buy my men faster cars. Then again, Liam has insisted that he'll take care of Gemma's protection.

I laugh at the thought. I don't consider the Irishman to be good at much of anything, let alone protecting his wife.

"Make me a deal," I tell Gemma. "Behave, only go to the Alibi, and don't ditch them."

"What do I get?" she retorts. "Deals should benefit both parties, Gian."

"A favor." I wave my hand dismissively. "You can bank it for later."

That seems to please her, a small smile rising on her cheeks. "Deal," she says, extending her hand for me to shake.

I don't like the idea of Rhea running off with my sister, especially knowing that the news of our engagement is out. Surely people will be watching her, hoping to catch her doing something to use against my

Chapter Seven

RHEA

Getting out of Gian's clutches is at the top of my to-do list. As soon as Gemma turns away from her brother, a grin growing on her face, I'm relieved.

Being near Gian boils my blood. The smug asshole walks through the place expecting everyone to worship at his feet. His confidence is far too high for my liking. Every time he comes near me, he wraps a hand around my waist or presses his palm against the small of my back. His actions shout to the room that he owns me now.

His eyes are glued to me. It feels like an invisible leash is wrapped around my throat, anchoring me to the mob boss. I yearn to break free, To rip off my chains and run as fast as I can.

But as much as being near Gian boils my blood, a glance at

my father makes me want to curl up next to my monster of a fiancé. If the choice is between one of the two devils standing before me, I'll choose Gian every time.

Someone else might say to stick with the devil you know, but I've lived with my father for fifteen years, long enough to tell me if I don't marry Gian he'll send me off to marry someone else. And at least with Gian I'll stay in Providence and I can practice law. It's not everything I've ever wanted, but it's better than the alternatives.

"We have babysitters," Gemma tells me, a slight frown marring her painted red lips. "But, at least he didn't say no."

My eyes drift from my friend's face back to her brother's, finding his dark orbs still trained on me. He looks at me like he sees more than anyone else. Those dark eyes pierce my skin, penetrating all the wards I've put in place to guard me from the fucked up world I live in. But he sees past that.

And it fucking terrifies me.

Gemma takes me to a bar owned by her brothers, the only option given by Gian. That's the thing with men like my new fiancé, they give you an inch, an inch that you're overly grateful for. They give you the taste of freedom, the idea that you're not tied down, but it's all an illusion.

We're in a club that he owns. A glance around shows cameras that probably feed directly to his phone or his brother's. Two men lean against a wall not far behind us, their eyes trained on us. They're close and it makes me wonder if I walk to the bathroom, will they follow me?

Everything here is under Gian's control.

Including me now.

"Drink," Gemma tells me, thrusting a shot glass of clear liquid in my direction.

My stomach sinks thinking about my new arrangement with her brother. Anxiety gathers there, filling me as my mind races through thoughts of having to spend my life with this man. It's the right choice, the only choice. Nevertheless, the idea of having to marry someone I don't love, or even really like, makes me want to vomit all over the Louboutin's on my feet.

I snatch the shot glass from Gemma's fingers, downing the clear liquid quickly. A surprised look washes over her features. "Okay," she says. "We need more shots!" She flags down the bartender with a flick of her wrist.

The one good thing about coming to a bar owned by the DelGado brothers is that the service is impeccable. As soon as Gemma lifts a finger, a bartender is in front of us. He pours more vodka into two clean glasses and sets them gently before us. "Anything else, Mrs. DelGado?" The man asks.

"O'Connor." She corrects with a smile and his face flushes immediately.

"My mistake," he apologizes quickly.

The look on his face has me wondering how Gian has instilled so much fear into his employees. What does he do, beat them for every mistake? Cut off limbs for messing up a drink?

Why is this town so afraid of the man?

As if answering my question, I see the man's eyes flicker to the one of the TV's mounted in the bar. Whipping my head to see the screen right as an image of a car explodes. The volume is too low to hear anything, but the subtitles tell me all I need to know.

Mayor killed in an assumed mob hit.

"Turn that off." Gemma waves to the man once she sees where my eyes have landed.

But turning it off doesn't erase the image from my brain.

The channel flickers and suddenly a basketball game plays out on the screen, but my head is still fixated on the explosion, the image of that car bursting into flames.

I'm marrying a murderer.

Gemma plies me with more shots and I wonder if it's because she knows the turmoil that's filling my brain, the anxiety that wrecks my heart. The shots come one after another until my mind has a nice film over it, making everything slightly blurry. My body is coated in a sheen of sweat as my hips move on the dance floor. Gemma waves her arms while facing me, her hips swaying along to whatever song blares from the speakers.

Dancing reminds me of my mother. The apartment we lived in before she passed away was tiny, a shoe box compared to my father and Elena's home, but the limited space meant little to her. She would turn the small living room into a dance floor. Blasting music from the stereo while she taught me how to move my body. I can practically feel her hands on my hips as I move them with the rhythm, hear her whispers as I listen to the beat.

Normally I get drunk to drown out the memories of her, of the life that no longer exists. But as I dance in the crowded bar, I feel her with me. Her presence drifting over me and bringing me a small amount of comfort.

Patrons crowd the bar and bump into us as they move from one end to the other. Hands grip onto my hips and I'm pulled backward until my ass meets someone else's groin. I'm thrown off by the action, not quite understanding what just happened.

My gaze rises to meet Gemma's eyes, who looks past me to whoever is now holding me in place. Her eyes tell me it's not Gian. The offender's lips come to my ears as he whisper-yells to me.

"You're fucking gorgeous," the stranger tells me.

It takes effort in my drunk state, too much effort, for me to spin myself around to face the offender. I tear his fingers from my hips, tossing his hands away from me like something dirty.

My being offended at his touch has nothing to do with my newfound fiancé and everything to do with not wanting this strange man to touch me. I can't understand what it is about men thinking they can grab whatever and whoever they want. As if women aren't people who get a choice in the matter.

Shock crosses the man's face; as if this is truly a revelation, he's surprised that I wouldn't want his grabby hands on my body.

"What the fuck do you think you're doing?" I ask.

He runs a hand through his hair while his glassy eyes rake

over me. I feel dirty just from his look.

"Appreciating you," he says and it takes all my willpower not to vomit in my mouth.

"Don't fucking touch me," I shoot back, but the liquor slurs my words and instead of backing away like he should, the man only comes closer, a smile spreading across his thin lips as his hand reaches back out to grab me.

"Don't touch me—" I'm cut off as he pulls me closer to him, shushing me as he does.

"I think she told you to back the fuck up," a deep voice rumbles from behind me and for the first time, I'm happy to hear Gian. When I turn around, he pulls me into his hip with a single arm. Protecting and stabilizing me.

"Yeah?" The stranger questions and I wince at his mistake. Gian's arm tightens around me as he speaks. "Why? You think you own the bitch?"

My fiancé chuckles softly, which doesn't seem to phase the man. He obviously doesn't know who Gian is or how much power he wields over this city. He says nothing for a moment, before finally settling on, "Have a good night."

The whole encounter felt like it lasted hours, but the alcohol has blurred time and I know it's really only been a few minutes. Gian drags me away with him and from the corner of my eye I see Gemma following closely behind.

"Nick," he says sternly as we reach the two men that have been watching us all night. "Take my sister home. Andrew, watch that prick and call me the second he leaves this bar. Do you *understand* me?" The way he emphasizes the word *understand* rattles my stomach. A look passes between the two men.

Once he's satisfied, Gian wraps his arm back around my waist and leads me out of the bar through the back exit. I barely have a second to yell goodbye at Gemma before the cool Providence air hits my skin. In fluid motions, he ushers me in his BMW and straps me into the passenger seat.

I settle into the buttery smooth leather as he rounds the car. He's silent as he buckles himself in and pulls us onto the road.

My head is blank. I don't know what to say to him. Sorry isn't in my vocabulary, especially not with the vodka running through my system. Plus, I don't for a second believe it was my fault. The feminist in me wants to scream at him for daring to protect me. I'm not a weak woman, definitely not the type of woman he's used to dealing with.

"If you yell at me for stepping in, you won't like what I have to say."

I purse my lips at his arrogance. Of course he would say that. He probably sees me as a damsel in distress and himself as the fucking hero.

Men love weak women.

"Why's that?" I ask, crossing my arms over my body.

"You can defend yourself, I know that."

I ease at his words, the anger slowly melting from me. "Then why—"

"You're mine, Rhea. And I don't give a fuck how strong and self-sufficient you are, if someone touches what's mine, I'll kill them."

He doesn't chuckle. Doesn't mutter. Doesn't even flinch at his words.

One hand is draped over the steering wheel as he navigates the roads efficiently. He's completely serious.

"You don't own me," I say, glossing over the fact that he said he would kill a man for touching me. It should bother me more than it does. Even with his serious tone, I don't think he'd be stupid enough to kill the man, not to mention that we've already left. The biggest concern for me at the moment is that this man thinks he owns me. Like I'm a possession that he can claim or trade.

A soft chuckle leaves his lips. "Whatever you want to believe, babe."

The pet names grate on me. "You don't!" I counter, raising my voice this time. It's a shitty argument and it only makes him laugh more, but it's all I can come up with in my drunken state.

"Oh Rhea, darling, that ring wrapped around your finger says otherwise."

Chapter Eight

GIAN

I put a drunk Rhea to bed in my condo. She fought me once I pulled into my parking lot. She didn't want to stay here or with me, but mentioning her father silenced her pretty quickly.

I can't blame her, I'm not sure I'd want to deal with Joe either. He has an air of superiority surrounding him. It's suffocating and I've spent a fraction of the time Rhea has with him. Joe has a good business sense, but not enough for him to act the way he does.

Rhea shrinks around him. Even with her smart ass responses and aloof gaze, I can still see her retracting, shying away whenever her father is near.

I make a mental note to dig into their relationship, figure out what makes the pair so hostile.

She changed into one of my t-shirts and a pair of shorts far too large for her in the privacy of my en suite bathroom. The shyness was a pleasant contrast to the bold Rhea who just cussed me out in the car earlier.

But as soon as her head hit the pillow, she was out. Perfect timing, really. As her breathing steadied, my phone vibrated with a text from Andrew. He followed the asshole home to a nice apartment in College Hill.

Now I was going to pay him a visit.

I slide back into the BMW and head out of the city toward College Hill. Unlike my sister, I never went to college at the esteemed Brown University on the other side of the hill. While my high school classmates were off studying literature and drinking in dorm rooms, I was working the streets, putting money in my pocket.

My father held the second most coveted position in *La Famiglia,* as the consigliere the boss's family was practically an extension of mine. As a kid I spent most of my time with Massimo's son Theo and the underbosses son Vinny.

Theo, Vinny, and I ran the streets as teenagers. We dealt every drug you could possibly think of and Massimo loved it. He loved having three young boys to do his bidding out in the city. It was well known that Providence was mafia territory, but most of the old guys have lived up on Federal Hill since they were kids.

Once Theo, Vinny, and I turned eighteen, we moved into the city, making it known that this territory was ours. Suddenly, less scum from Boston tried to move in on our streets. It was a win for everybody.

We were just happy to be on his good side.

Experience taught us that being on his shit list never ended well.

The fucker's apartment complex is nicer than I wanted to admit, not that him living in a shithole would make a difference. People in shitty apartments are just less likely to call the cops.

I see Andrew's Escalade as I pull up. He doesn't leave the vehicle when I arrive, instead he waits for me to call his phone, staying as unnoticeable as possible.

"He hasn't left. Apartment one-oh-eight," the kid answers. Andrew is only nineteen years old, but the kid is loyal and far more responsible than I was at his age.

"Good," I answer.

"Ya want me to stay here, boss?" Andrew asks. The kid is eager to get in on some action, that much I know, but this fucker is mine.

"Nah, I got this." I slip on a pair of black leather gloves as I slide out of the BMW.

So much for staying under the radar.

The door to his apartment is open, making it easy for me to sneak into the place without the jackass even knowing. I find him in the back, stepping out of the pair of jeans he had been wearing and standing by his bed in only a white undershirt and boxers.

"What the fuck?" His face turns into a confused frown when he looks up to find me standing in the doorway. "What the hell are you doing here?"

I don't waste time, stalking forward and landing a punch to his right eye, the action makes both of his hands fly to his face, protecting the eye socket.

"Teaching you a lesson, you little shit!" I growl, landing another hit on the other eye.

Massimo trained me to be a fighter. I haven't fought anyone since I was in my early twenties. Eventually the need to show dominance through the pounding of my fists faded away. But the skills are still ingrained into me.

The fucker in front of me isn't even trying though, he's too busy protecting his precious face. I strike again, this time landing a hit on his nose causing the bone to crunch beneath my knuckles.

"Fuck!" he screams, but the word barely penetrates the bubble I'm in, surrounded by memories instead of being in the moment.

Suddenly, I'm no longer in the nice apartment in College Hill, the room has morphed into a basement I haven't seen in years. The pale walls have turned to cinder block with a cement floor under my feet. Instead of the asshole from the bar, it's another piece of scum beneath me.

I can hear Massimo screaming in my ears. "End it," he growls at me. "If you can't kill this piece of trash with your bare hands, you'll never be worthy of being a made man."

And just like that night, my hands gravitate to the man's neck, gripping around the sensitive flesh and squeeze. He struggles underneath my palms, his arms reaching forward and clawing at my skin. I don't feel a thing, not a single thing until the last gasp leaves his lips and his body slacks beneath my grip.

A breath escapes my own lips as my mind clears and I remember where I am.

"Shit," I mutter.

I killed the fucker.

There are droplets of blood speckling my glove, trailing up the sleeves of my shirt.

I'm not sure at what point I broke his skin, but the cuts on his face drip with red fluid. "Fuck." I wasn't supposed to go this far. I'm supposed to be cool and collected, but something about this fucker touching what's mine brought out the worst in me.

I make my way to the sink in his bathroom, scrubbing the remnants of his blood from my skin, careful to wipe down every surface that I touch.

Plucking the cell phone from inside my suit jacket, I make a call to Andrew. "Boss," he answers on the first ring.

"I need you in here. We've got to clean the place."

He doesn't respond for a moment and when he does, surprise laces his words. "He's dead?"

I scrub a hand down my face, ignoring Andrew's question. I've told the kid a handful of times not to kill when a few well placed punches can do the trick. Murder is a whole different ball game, it requires planning and cleanup. No wonder he's shocked at my spontaneous kill.

"I'll be there in a second," Andrew adds when I don't answer his question, ending the call.

I dial Gio next. "What?" he answers on the second ring, his voice weary and sleep deprived. My brother has been trying to be an active father, taking turns staying up with his baby. The role has left him crankier than normal.

"I need you to go to Alibi. I have a bag in the safe marked B1, I need you to bring that to the location I'm about to send you."

"What's going on?" he asks, the sleepiness leaving his voice.

I sigh heavily, staring at myself in the bathroom mirror. "I made a mistake, but I'm fixing it."

"Okay," Gio says, no more questions asked. "I'll be there soon."

Andrew is in the house already, pulling a pair of black leather gloves onto his hands. "Where do you want me to start?" he asks. "Want me to wrap the body?"

"No, leave the body. We're staging the scene."

It's almost dawn by the time I get back to my condo. Every inch of my body aches and my mind is foggy and tired. I almost forget about Rhea in my bed until I break through the bedroom door to her sleeping form.

She's cute like this, when she's passed out and quiet. I know she'll give me hell for climbing into bed with her, but there's no way I'm sleeping on the couch after the night I just had. First, I shower, needing to wash the remnants of that asshole from my body.

Discarding my clothing, I step into the scalding spray of my rainforest shower, letting the water wash away the memories of his skin smacking beneath my fists. Of his bones crunching from my punches. I let the vision of his hands on Rhea's body trickle down the drain with the water.

Assuming Rhea won't want to wake up to a naked version of me, I pull on a pair of form fitting boxers once I'm dry and climb under the down comforter with her. I've never been one for cuddling, but the sight of her curled up next to me with her locks of dark hair fanned out over the pillow makes me want to wrap an arm around her. I have the sudden desire to find out what her body feels like pressed up against mine.

Jesus, I need to calm the fuck down. I roll over and close my eyes, hoping sleep comes soon.

When I wake up, it's with her body curled into mine. I don't know when, but at some point I must have wrapped an arm around her, pulling her close to me. She shifts under my arm, turning her head slightly and meeting my gaze. Her green eyes are coated with sleep, blinking rapidly as she looks at me.

"What?" she asks. "How did I get here?"

I chuckle. I should have known. She was drunker than I would have liked last night. Alcohol is a weakness, one my sister enjoys too much. I prefer to remain with my wits about me. I like to be sharp and be able to handle any crisis that arises. Alcohol dulls all the senses.

"You were drunk," I tell her. "I took you home."

Realization comes over her and she drags a hand to her face, shielding herself from me. "The man at the bar?"

"Yeah," I say. "You were pretty annoyed with me for helping you."

The hand drops from her face as those green eyes pierce me. "You said *you owned me*." The words leave her lips with a bitter, accusing taste.

"You say that like it's a bad thing, *cara*."

"I'm a person, Gian, not a car. You can't *own* me."

In one swift movement I roll her over so she's on her back and I'm balancing above her, pinning her arms to the mattress beneath us. "You're mine, *cara mia,* I told you then and I'll tell you now, no one touches what's mine."

She wiggles beneath my grip, straining to remove her forearms from my grasp. "You didn't do much last night," she growls, showing her teeth. "You just smiled and let him be."

I grin, my little darling doesn't know that the big bad wolf doesn't have a temper. You can't just put someone in their place in broad daylight, and definitely not with the FBI agent sitting a few feet away at the bar.

No, you need a plan.

"You don't need to worry about him anymore, I took care of it last night."

Her face freezes. "What the fuck does that mean?"

"It means, the idiot who thought to put his hands on your body is dead."

An icy look creeps over her, stilling all of her features and locking her eyes on me. Her wrists are completely still under my grip.

For a smart woman, who grew up in this fucked up world, she has no idea how it actually works.

"You killed him." The words escape from her lips in a hushed whisper.

I lift one arm, pushing my weight onto my elbow so I can stroke her hair with my hand in a soothing gesture. "What did you think would happen, baby? You think I'd let anyone touch what's mine and then walk out of my club with no repercussions?" I hiss under my breath. "Silly girl, I've killed men for less."

She wiggles beneath me, trying to escape from my grip. The friction feels too good against me and I have to fight myself to keep from growing hard at the motion.

"You're a monster," she hisses.

"Maybe," I tell her, "But I never promised to be Prince Charming."

Chapter Nine

RHEA

"Oooh!" Elena squeals as we enter the bridal shop. At least one of us is excited about wedding dress shopping. She's immediately drawn to a rack of frilly white gowns, plucking one with far too much tulle from the display and fawning over it.

I haven't seen my fiancé in weeks and our last meeting still plays in my head in a sick loop. I can't stop thinking about the fact that a man is dead for doing nothing more than getting handsy with me at a bar. If Gian knew about every man who had dared to touch me, or barge into my personal space, there would be bodies lining the streets of Providence.

I can't imagine what he would do to the men who I willingly let into my bedroom. Those men whose hands have touched me in places I'll never allow Gian access to. He would go on a murder spree if he knew all the dirty things that have brought me pleasure.

I shudder at the thought.

For a fake marriage, the asshole is quite the control freak.

"What are we looking for today?" A far too pleasant blonde woman asks, a silly question I think since the shop exclusively sells wedding dresses. She smoothes her hands down the plum fitted dress she's wearing.

"My daughter is getting married," Elena gushes.

The only bright spot of dress shopping is seeing the excitement on Elena's face. She met me in my room the night Gian sprung the engagement on me with a plate of cookies and a bottle of wine. There's not much more I could want in a stepmother. She held me while I cried and then told me everything would be okay. Even if I didn't believe her, I appreciated the kind words.

The woman introduces herself as Kate and smiles brightly while Elena talks about the wedding plans, the ceremony and elaborate party to be held in two months. Extremely fast considering I've been engaged for two weeks, but Gian wanted it 'as soon as possible' and Elena is a 'yes' woman.

Within days, she had the venue booked and the other details fell into place. Apparently a rushed wedding is easy to plan when you get to use the weight of the DelGado name.

I was happy to let her plan her dream wedding. I wanted nothing to do with the whole arrangement. Preferably, we'd get married in a courthouse and just be done with the entire ordeal. But both of our families wanted extravagant parties, events to show off to their friends and all of Providence.

My father is thrilled about my pending nuptials. The idea of being that close to power is too alluring to him.

"A train," I hear Elena saying to Kate, snapping me out of my head.

"No," I cut in. "No trains. Please."

Elena frowns. "Are you sure?"

The one thing I don't think I can handle is an enormous dress. No tulle, no trains. I'd prefer not to look like a marshmallow up in a giant gown walking down the church aisle.

"Simple," I say. "Can I just do something simple?"

Elena caves, sending off the woman to bring us a selection of simple but elegant gowns.

"I know you're not thrilled about this," Elena says when it's just the two of us. "But I want you to be happy, Rhe." She's genuine when she says this. Elena has never been the evil stepmother. If anything, she's been the best part of moving in with my father.

While I'd never claim that Elena's a strong woman, she shrinks next to my father and isn't one to fight for what she wants, I can definitely say that she's always had my back.

"Thank you…" I trail. "It's just not ideal."

"He seems nice," she tells me, it's something she's said before, an attempt at soothing me.

"I don't think Gian DelGado is nice," I mutter.

She swats my shoulder playfully. "He's not a bad guy," she tries, but I frown at her. It's a terrible choice of wording because

I'm pretty sure we both know he is. Elena isn't a stupid woman, she knows exactly what her husband does to support us, she just doesn't care. Or she justifies it by finding ways to believe that some amount of bad if done for good reasons or some bullshit.

I figured out exactly what kind of man my father was early on after moving in with them. Maybe it was because I had ten years without him, I could see him clearly where Christopher and Elena had too much history clouding their vision.

He gambled, cheated, and came home with lipstick stains on his collar. There were moments when Elena cursed and swatted at him, when I thought she'd fight back. But somehow he always turned it around to be her fault. Letting her know everything she'd done that made him go out and find someone else to warm his bed. He used his fists to get his way, painting her body with intricate bruises until she gave up on fighting.

Their arguments made me sick to my stomach.

Elena accepted that kind of half-assed love, but I swore to myself I never would.

Somehow I didn't believe that Gian would be better than my father.

Kate comes back, filling the rack outside the dressing room with a selection of gowns. Elena loves every single one she touches, oohing and ahhing at each of the dresses.

I land on one. A simple silk A-line gown that reaches the floor with no train. It has an elegant neckline and long sleeves. The back of the dress dips low, the only scandalous feature of the dress. I try it on first, sliding the soft material up my body.

I've never been the type of woman to fantasize about a dress. But if I ever did, this would be it.

When I exit the dressing room, Elena's eyes move over the dress, her lower lashes pooling with water. "It's beautiful," she whispers.

I don't know if it's right or wrong to say this about the first dress, but "This is the one."

"I hear you bought a dress."

I'm sucked into my work when Gian enters my office. The file in front of me is for a client I know damn well Giuseppe won't take on. The man sticks exclusively to easy to win cases or ones that bring in big money. When he's not handling cases for made men or those affiliated with the organization.

Every once in a while a case comes in that doesn't fit his norm. A woman abused by her husband, sex workers victimized on the city streets, women hurting and needing help. I can't say that Giuseppe doesn't feel bad for these women, because I think he does, he just doesn't want to take their cases.

"Hard to win," he'll mutter to himself, stamping the intake form with the word decline and tossing it back to Gemma or Edie to call the poor girl.

The one I'm reading now is from a nineteen-year-old college student. She was brutally raped, drunk beyond the point of blacking out. Tears welled in my eyes as I read what she said to

Gemma on the phone.

I need help.

How terrible are we for denying a woman begging to be helped? To be heard?

"What are you reading?" Gian asks when I don't respond. He crosses my office in seconds, yanking the paper from my fingertips and scanning his eyes over the document. "My father won't take this case," he says, dropping the paper and letting the sheets flutter back down to my desk.

His eyes find mine and I know he's seeing the water that's gathering on my lower lash line. His demeanor changes for a moment, softens at my emotion.

"I don't think I've ever seen you sad," he mutters. "Angry as hell, but never sad."

"What do you want?" I ask hastily, wiping the stray tears from my eyes.

"There she is." He smirks at my change in attitude. "Why does this upset you, anyway?" he asks, eyes flickering to the intake form.

"Why doesn't it upset you?" I retort.

My sass only makes him grin wider. "Careful, *cara*, you're being emotional," he chides.

"Fuck you." I stand from my desk chair, smoothing down my pencil skirt and crossing my arms. "You can leave now."

Slipping his hands into his pockets, he let his eyes scan over my body, taking in the fitted skirt and tucked in blouse. Gian's not shy about admiring my looks, every encounter I've had with him has included his eyes scanning my body.

"Don't be dramatic," he says, a laugh following his demeaning words.

Men like to call women dramatic anytime they show an inkling of emotion. I frown at the words and the asshole attitude that my soon-to-be husband sports.

"It's not dramatic, Gian. It's a woman's life. How can you be so dismissive?"

He scrubs a hand through his slicked back hair, ruffling it; my eyes focus on the out of place strands imagining them as chips in his perfectly placed armor.

"So what? Are you telling me you want to represent this girl?" His thick eyebrows raise, questioning me. "You haven't even passed the bar exam."

I know he's not naïve, he knows damn well that Gemma and I have been meeting with clients, connecting them to lawyers who will support them and helping them pay their legal fees with money we've raised from generous donations. The only man in her family who hasn't donated to our cause is the one in front of me.

"You can't save everyone, Rhea. It's naïve to try."

"So I should give up?" I ask, fighting the urge to throw up my hands or let tears fall from my eyes. I'm stronger than that, I've spent years building up my defenses, strengthening myself against men like this, men who don't believe in me. "Is this what

I have to look forward to in our marriage? Constant doubts and no support from my husband?"

A scoff escapes his lips as his dark eyes drill into me. "I didn't come here to fight with you."

"I would have guessed otherwise."

We stand there in silence for an elongated moment, both of us studying the other one, both waiting for the other to break the silence.

A harsh breath leaves Gian's lips as he speaks first. "Truce?" he asks and I think this might be the first time Gian DelGado has ever not gotten his way with someone. "I don't want you to hate me," he mutters. "So if this makes you happy, you should do it."

"Thank you for your permission, *sir,*" I scoff. "But I'm already doing it."

Smoldering eyes glare at me. "Rhea," he admonishes. "I'm trying to work with you, but I can't do that when you're acting like a stuck-up bitch."

Red coats my vision at his use of the word bitch. "You fucking asshole."

He's on me in seconds, stalking forward while I move back until he has me pressed up against the wall. His body meets mine, thick muscles pressing into my stomach, sandwiching me between the wall of my office and the man I'm betrothed to.

"Tell me what you want, *cara,*" he breathes low into my ear, the tone sending a spark of electricity through me.

How am I possibly attracted to this asshole?

"I-what?" I mutter, my brain no longer working with him this close to me. All of my witty remarks have flown out the window. He invades my space and takes over my brain, filling it with thoughts that are no longer laced with hate. Primal fucking urges replace my rage as his dark and spicy scent fills my nostrils.

"Negotiate with me," he says, a smile drawing up on his lips. "Tell me what you want and we can come to a deal. You want money, a donation? Tell me what will make you fucking happy, Rhea?" His lips graze along my ear as he says the words.

Multiple emotions swirl through my head. Do I hate him too much not to make a deal? To take him up on his offer? How much money can I ask for from this man? Is it wrong to take money from a murderer, even if I'm using it to help others?

"Hmm..." He goads me, "What will it be?"

"A million?" I ask, going for a bigger number, willing myself to take the blood money to help others, like the woman whose intake form sits on my desk.

A sinister smile tugs at his lips. "Done," he whispers.

Shock washes over me. Did he really just agree to a million dollars?

"And... what do you want from me then?" I ask, terrified of his answer.

"I want you to fucking smile when you walk down the aisle."

Chapter Ten

GIAN

FBI agent prime suspect in College Hill murder investigation. It takes longer than I expected for the headline to hit the news. They keep Agent Baldwin's name out of the papers, his identity under wraps, a courtesy my men are never given. I run a hand through the scruff that's been settling on my face. I'm long past due for a shave, too enthralled with the news on my TV and the revolving door of problems brought to my office to get a good shave.

Gio drops an electric razor on my desk and slumps into the seat across from me. "Ya know," he begins, the tips of his fingers tracing over his chin. "If they figure out you set him up, it's going to mean war."

"It's already war," I shoot back. The FBI was gunning for me before I ever stepped foot into that apartment, before I ever strategically placed Agent Baldwin's fingerprints all over the scene. Fingerprints he so stupidly left on a mug of coffee at my restaurant.

The thought brings a smile to my lips. That asshole and the mayor underestimated me. And now look where they are.

One is six feet under and the other is soon to be a prison inmate.

"You're fucked up, ya know that." He grimaces. "That's the FBI you're fucking with."

My lips curl upward, the smile on my face widening. "I know, brother. I needed to send a message and now I have."

"And your message is that you want to die, huh?" Gio shakes his head before his dark eyes find mine again. "What's the endgame here?" he asks earnestly.

"Winning," I tell him. "The city is still reeling from Massimo's death, our men are still suffering, the streets have trust issues. When this is over, money will line our pockets and the *Famiglia* will be happy."

"Okay." He nods. "Whatever you need, brother, I'll take care of it. Or I'll get someone on it, but you need to fucking distance yourself from this. If this murder comes back to you, you're screwed."

My brother is not wrong and it's a line my father has been spouting for months. The boss should sit behind a desk, making decisions and giving orders to his closest men. Only the legal businesses should stay in my name, everything else needs to go. I need layers between me and what happens on the streets of Providence. So many layers that it's impossible to trace anything back to me. I know this.

Still, I'm the type of man that likes to get my hands dirty.

Two knocks rap on my office door before Rafi opens. "Boss," he says, "She's here."

Rhea, the she in question, storms past Rafi, her heels tapping aggressively on the hardwood. "Are you kidding me?" she asks, crossing her arms over her chest.

Rafi backs out of the office quietly, shutting the door as he goes.

"Rhea," I purr, leaning back in my seat and bringing my gaze to meet hers.

My brother leans away from the raging woman who just stormed into my office, an amused expression washing over his features. He lifts a single hand, placing it strategically over his lips to hide the smile growing on his face.

"You can't just summon me," she growls. My bride looks vicious, even in her fitted pencil skirt and high heels. She's the perfect image of a working woman. The kind you see sitting at the head of the table in a boardroom, running the whole damn company. She looks fucking powerful.

"I called."

My retort only makes the fury burn stronger in her gaze. "And

I didn't answer, so you had one of your cronies come to my office and drag me out kicking and screaming?" Her voice rises as she continues to speak. "Is that the foundation of our relationship?" she yells, her hands slap the curves of her hips as she berates me.

Slowly, I rise from my desk, brushing off my suit and standing up. I stalk over to her at an easy pace. "Gio, you want to give us a moment?"

"Gladly," he replies, jumping out of his seat. "Nice to see you again, Rhea." He smiles softly before getting out of my office as fast as he can.

I take another slow step toward Rhea. She doesn't back down, instead standing strongly before me until we're chest to chest. Her green eyes peer up at me, waiting for my response.

"There's a solution to this problem," I tell her coolly. "Answer your damn phone."

The intensity of the rage swirling in those green orbs only grows stronger as we stand there staring at each other, neither one of us willing to break. You could cut through the tension with a knife.

There's an unspoken game being played between us and both of us want to win. Both of us want to assert control and power over the other. It sets the tone for our marriage, the winner clearly being the one in charge, and each of us are eager to have that power.

"You can't possibly expect me to come when called. I'm not a dog, Gian, I'm a fucking human and you will treat me with respect." She growls the words at me and I let her.

I let her go off on her tangent, let her get it all out of her system, and when she finishes, I push her so her back hits the wall behind her. While she's busy being shocked, I grab both of her wrists, lifting her arms and pinning them over her head with one hand before using the other to grab her chin, holding it in place so she's looking at me.

"Listen to meme, Rhea, and listen well because I won't repeat myself. When I call, you answer. Do you understand ?"

I feel her inhale deeply through her nose, that look of stubborn rage ever present on her face. She doesn't respond, her lips staying pressed in a thin line.

"Rhea," I coo, "Answer me."

She blinks for a long moment as I feel the control slip from her. "Yes," she whispers, finally submitting to me.

"Good girl," I murmur, dropping her hands.

Immediately she grabs her wrists, rubbing them as if they're in pain, even though I know I barely squeezed them. "What did you even want?" she mutters, her gaze avoiding me. She's pissed and I get that. She wants to be the strongest one in the room, probably has been her entire life. But that's not how it's going to work with me and the sooner she realizes that, the better it will be for her.

"Pick a house," I tell her, dropping a manila folder at the edge of my desk.

Tentatively she reaches for it, opening the folder to reveal three packets, each with pictures and details on different houses. I narrowed it down for her but decided I would let her have the final say, call it a wedding present or something.

Tears well in her eyes as she flips through the houses I picked, but a look at her lips still pressed thin tells me the tears aren't from overwhelming gratitude.

"What?" I ask, harsher than I mean to. I'm not sure why the packet of multi-million dollar mansions I put in front of her is making her cry in a bad way.

Green eyes flash to mine, and I think she's trying to prevent herself from giving me a dirty look. "Nothing," she mutters. "It doesn't matter, whatever you decide." She drops the folder back onto my desk.

I breathe in sharply, pinching the bridge of my nose in annoyance. I don't know what she wants. Marriage doesn't come with a rule book and I wasn't made for this. I was trained to be a killer, a money maker, but never a husband.

"What do you want, Rhea?"

She wraps her arms around herself, avoiding my gaze. "I don't think my opinion matters," she whispers.

I wanted her to comply, to listen and do what I say. But now that all of her spark is gone, I miss it. I want the sassy version of Rhea back.

Can't I have the sass without the anger?

I scrub a hand over my face. "Okay," I mutter. "I'm sorry… if I offended you."

She blinks her eyes a few times, looking at me with shock. "You're confusing me, Gian. I don't know what you want from me." Her shoulders drop with defeat.

I don't know what I want from her either. I reacted impulsively with Rhea, tricking her into this arrangement because one look at her and I wanted her to be mine.

There have been plenty of woman I've wanted to fuck and I've put far less effort into them than I have with Rhea. If I truly just wanted a wife to appease my men, to solidify my status, surely there was a better choice than the woman in front of me. But one look at her sends electricity through my veins.

I never learned how to woo a woman because I was too busy learning to take what I wanted. And I wanted Rhea Cabrera.

I take a step toward her and this time she backs away from me willingly, her eyes as wide as saucers when I push against her this time.

Wordlessly, I bring my lips to hers, pressing a soft kiss to her mouth. I lick along the seam of her lips until she opens up for me and then I kiss her harder, more passionately. Her tongue wars against mine defiantly, that spark reigniting in her. She doesn't back away anymore, instead she meets me, kiss for kiss, war for war.

My hands drift over her body, feeling the swells of her breasts and curves of her hips. She lifts a leg, hooking it around my waist and pulling me even closer to her. One of my hands finds its way to her hair, tangling itself into the wild dark curls.

Without warning, her leg unwraps itself and her palms come to my chest, shoving me away from her. Her breath leaves her lips raggedly as she pants, her gaze no longer on mine. "What are we doing?" she asks softly.

I lick my lips, still tasting her, the scent of her honey lip-gloss tainting my skin and nostrils. She smells sweet, like citrus, and I want more of her. I want all of her.

"We're kissing." I say gruffly.

"You can't do that to me," she yells, straightening her posture. "You can't drag me here, yell at me, apologize, and kiss me. You're giving me fucking whiplash, Gian!" She tosses her hands up in the air. A heavy sigh leaves her lips. "You want a fake marriage? Fine. You want me to pretend in public, want me to host parties and be the perfect wife? Fine. But don't kiss me like that, because this is nothing but fake."

She spins on her heels, the handle of my office door already in her hand. "Can I leave now?" she asks, her eyes still trained ahead on the door, refusing to look at me.

"Yes," I mutter.

She doesn't say another word, instead she lets the clicks of her high heels do the talking as she waltzes out of my office.

Chapter Eleven

RHEA

I've gone to church every Sunday for as long as I can remember. It was the one thing that never changed moving from my mother's apartment to my father's home. Both of them valued a steady relationship with their maker.

Today's visit to the church where I've spent every Sunday of my life feels different though.

This time, it feels like a weight strapped around my ankle, keeping me trapped in place. Enslaved to this town. Chained to a man with dark hair and icy veins. My chest feels tight when I think about walking down the aisle to meet my soon-to-be husband.

There's a fury of motion around me, women piled into my house to help me get ready. I have more bridesmaids than I know what to do with. Elena's nieces, Gian's cousins, and of course Gemma.

My wedding day is nothing like I imagined. Not that I was the type of girl who grew up imagining lavish or extravagant weddings. I never had a Pinterest board filled with frilly white dresses. I didn't dream about this day for half of my life.

Elena woke me up early to start my hair and makeup, even though the ceremony doesn't start until early afternoon. My eyes feel heavy, tired from not being able to sleep the night before. I couldn't stop the anxiety about my new life from filling my head. My anger toward Gian is still sizzling inside of me, despite not having seen him in days. I like it better this way, the further away he is, the less I have to think of him.

I'm trying to smile, trying to be positive or happy, but the emotion doesn't come easy to me. The desire to escape nags at my soul and it takes every ounce of effort in me to keep my feet planted.

"Drink," Gemma says, handing me a glass of champagne with a drop of orange juice. "You look nervous."

I take the glass thankfully. "I'm not," I say, but it's a bold face lie and we both know it. I'm practically shaking. Marrying Gian DelGado is not the dream for me. I'm meant to do more than be a trophy wife, I know this.

I wonder what my mom would think of me if she was here. Would she have wanted this path for me? My chest tightens at the thought of her. My childhood idolization of her says she would have wanted me to marry for love and not for status. She would have rather I be happy and poor than rich and miserable.

But then again, she was with my father and no part of me believes that my mother, my idol, loved a man as terrible as him.

Of course, I'll never know the truth, never know why she was with him.

Maybe love makes you do stupid things.

I glance over at Elena, who's smiling and laughing with one of her sisters as they have their makeup done. Elena is far too nice for my father. Too sweet, too caring. Why did she marry him?

I know one thing for a fact. If Gian and I ever manage to produce children, I will never put them in this situation. I would let him kill me before he forced my daughter to marry a man she didn't love.

Gemma sighs heavily beside me. "He wasn't always like this, ya know," she whispers and it takes me a moment to realize who she's talking about. "He was sweet, as a kid, I mean. He was a good big brother."

"What changed?" I ask, downing a gulp of champagne, letting the alcohol take the edge off.

She shrugs. "There were a bunch of us kids, three of our families, ya know. Gio, Adelina, and I were younger, plus Addy and I were girls so we weren't driven as hard. But Gian was the oldest. Uncle Massimo took interest in him, he used to train him, Theo, and Vinny. He'd come home with cuts and bruises. One time a broken arm." She looks up at me, her brown eyes glossy. "I don't know what he did to Gian, he never spoke of it, but I know something happened. I know he pitted them against each other, and now the only one left alive is Gian. I won't say he's a good guy, not after everything he's done to me. But deep down, somewhere in there is a decent person, I think." She squeezes my hand, looking away for a moment. "It will be okay."

"He gave us a million dollars," I say.

Gemma's eyes widen and her head whips around to face me again. "What?"

"He asked me what I wanted and I said a million dollars for our non-profit. The next day he sent me the login details for a new bank account and when I looked, it had a million dollars sitting in it. I didn't know what to say, so I just logged out of the account."

Gemma laughs loudly beside me, her face contorting with emotion. "Fuck," she gasps. "What did he ask for in return? There's always a motive."

I chuckle. "For me to smile when I walk down the aisle."

Gemma only laughs harder at that, the sound shaking her body. "You? With your resting bitch face?"

"Hey!" I punch her shoulder playfully. "Not cool."

Laughter is still bubbling out of her and she takes a moment to calm down before she looks at me again. "Listen," she says, this time more serious. "My brother isn't a great man, but he's a decent one. It's going to be okay. And if he does anything to hurt you, I will kill him. Or more likely, Liam will."

"Thank you," I tell her, bringing her in for a tight hug.

Now all I have to do is get through the wedding day.

I inhale a long breath of air as I walk up the steps to St. Patrick's Cathedral. Even before I moved in with my father, my mother would bring me to this same hall of worship. She would sit me down in the last row and listen to the priest spiel on and on. At the end she would get on her knees and pray, and tiny me would sit next to her wondering what the words she mouthed were. Wondering what she was praying for.

Even with its familiarity, the church aisle still haunts me. Elena has the place covered in flowers and lace. The colors are a spring green and a pale pink. With her décor, she made the old stuffy church look fresh and new.

My father looked shocked for a moment when he first saw me. There were no tears, no carefully photographed moments for us to look back on later. Our love is not that of a sweet father/daughter relationship, in our hearts we're still enemies. But for a second, I saw a flicker of emotion flow through him before it was quickly replaced with his normal icy look.

Elena cried when I had slid the dress up my body. The makeup artist had to do touch-ups to fix the look Elena had sobbed all over. A waste of effort, probably, because I'm sure she'll cry again as soon as the double doors at the back of the church open.

Seeing myself in the dress felt surreal. I couldn't imagine that the woman in my reflection was actually me. The idea that in a few hours I would be a married woman was nearly incomprehensible to me.

I never wanted this path for myself.

I never wanted to be the perfect wife. I never wanted to be a liar. To pretend to be something I'm not.

But in a few minutes Rhea Cabrera will cease to exist and in her place will stand Rhea DelGado, Queen of Providence.

I can't see it yet, but somewhere at the front of this church my groom stands with a line of men at his side.

Music blares from the string quartet Elena hired and my bridesmaids begin to waltz down the aisle. With each one that makes their way through the double doors, more panic settles in my stomach.

This is really happening.

Gemma is the last to go as my matron of honor. She tosses me a last smile before she begins her walk and once she reaches the end, the music shifts and all the guests rise to their feet.

The church is full, probably four to five hundred people are packed into the pews, all of their eyes staring at me.

I shouldn't be surprised when my father leads me down the aisle, but I am. Even knowing him as well as I do, the childish part of me still expects some kind of apology. Or a thank you.

But he's silent as he marches me down the aisle at a slow pace.

I meet Gian's eyes, focusing only on them as I continue my slow march. His dark eyes are focused on me and then slowly his lips turn up into an animated smile, only for a second, a reminder of my promise.

I curve my gloss coated lips into a big smile. Elena told me my signature red wasn't fitting for a bride. She wanted me to look more virginal and I wasn't going to be the one to tell her that ship had sailed a long time ago.

My father kisses my cheek and hands me off to Gian. The whole motion is supposed to be symbolic of his handing me over to my husband, but it feels transactional and too realistic. My leash is being tossed over to a new man and in return my father will make more money and have more power.

I'm just getting a new owner.

Gian takes my hand as I step up onto the chancel, meeting him and the priest.

"You look beautiful, *wife*."

My heart doesn't stop pounding in my chest the entire time the priest speaks. I go through the motions with a numbness spreading through my body. I go where I'm told, following my soon-to-be husband's lead. The ceremony feels like it will last forever, even though I know it's only an hour. An hour of Catholic traditions and prayers and finally our vows.

My mouth is dry when the priest asks me to repeat after him, and the words that leave my lips are so soft and quiet. Gian smiles at my discomfort. I think he gets off on my pain, enjoys watching me flinch.

When the priest announces Gian can 'kiss his bride,' my husband leans in slowly, bringing his lips to my mouth and pressing them against me softly. A hand sneaks around my waist,

117

pulling me closer as he dives into me. It's longer than a chaste kiss, he lets his tongue explore my mouth and when he finally pulls away, he has a soft smile on his face.

He brings his lips to my ear, "Remember to smile, *cara*."

And then steps back, looking out to the guests that fill the church, hundreds of people, with a grin on his face.

I try to match his enthusiasm, try to plaster a fake smile across my glossy lips, but I feel like a part of me has just died standing here at the front of the steps.

I clutch the glass of red wine between my fingertips, wondering if I can get out of this sham of a wedding if I spill the contents of the glass down the silky white dress. I can imagine the red liquid as it splashes, spreading along the smooth silk and soaking into the threads.

I find a sick pleasure in this fantasy.

"Rhea." the voice that interrupts my internal fantasy belongs to my new father-in-law. Giuseppe looks dapper in his three-piece black suit with a pair of shiny black loafers. His salt and pepper hair is slicked back and his face is clear of stubble. He has a wide grin on his cheeks as he pulls me into his embrace. When he leans back, his hands are still planted on my shoulders, holding me as he assesses.

His eyes are shiny under the lights of the ballroom. "I'm so happy," he tells me and the fractures in my heart crack a little at those words. "I'm so happy to have you in our family." He looks genuine when he says this, the smile pushing up to meet his eyes.

There are a lot of things I could say about Giuseppe DelGado. I don't love the men he raised for one. I hate the way he practices law. The way he takes only clients that will give him a large payday or the ones that got in legal trouble while doing Gian's bidding. I don't see him as a real attorney, more like a shoddy version of Saul Goodman.

But beneath all that, I think Giuseppe has a good heart. He means well, even if his execution isn't the best. And he loves his children, with his whole heart. I can't deny that.

I push my lips back up into a smile as I regard my new father-in-law. "Thank you, me too."

He chuckles softly, "I know you don't love my son."

His words catch me off guard. We all know this wedding is a farce, but mostly, it's unspoken. A secret that no one says out loud. We all pretend that Gian and I are madly in love, even if we all know that's a lie.

But Giuseppe outright saying it feels different.

"My wife and I loved our children very much," Giuseppe continues. "I never planned for any of them to get married in the ways they did," he laughs. "Gio with the pregnancy, Gemma with the Irish boy and now this... this arrangement." He pauses for a moment, letting his words sink in. "I wanted each of them to find love, real true love. Ya know, I loved Maria, my late wife. She was everything I ever wanted in a partner. Even after thirty something years, I loved coming home to her."

My mother never dated once she had me, never brought men home. I never saw her with someone, never learned how to accept love from watching her. I knew almost immediately that the love between my father and Elena was wrong. I never for a second believe that love manifested itself in the form of bruises and cracked ribs. I can't fathom what Giuseppe is trying to tell me, can't understand that love is more than a trade-off.

I never wanted to marry at all. And now, listening to my father-in-law talk about his late wife, I wonder if it was because I've never witnessed true love. I've never seen what a real partnership looks like.

And now I guess I never will.

"I wanted that for my kids," he says. "And I think they all found it in their own way, even if I wasn't thrilled with it." He swallows hard before bringing his eyes to meet mine. "I hope you and Gian find that. I know your marriage is unconventional, but I hope you can both find happiness." Giuseppe squeezes my shoulder in what I imagine is a fatherly way. "And if he ever lays a finger on you, you tell me, hmm? He's not too old for me to beat the shit out of." He chuckles deeply.

I don't know what to say. Tears coat my lashes. I've never had a man care about my feelings, care about my well-being. I don't know if he knows about my father, about the way he treats Elena and I, but his words mean more to me than I can articulate.

I choke back my tears. "Thank you."

Chapter Twelve

GIAN

I have to give my new mother-in-law credit, the wedding she planned single-handedly is actually pretty nice. And expensive.

She ran up quite the tab, but I couldn't complain. Not when my father wanted all the bells and whistles and I asked her to plan the thing on short notice.

Giuseppe looks happier than I've seen him since Ma's death. Ma would have loved today, and she and Elena would have gotten along exceptionally. Not to mention she would have cried seeing baby Gabriella dressed up in a tiny white dress with Annie helping her toss flowers down the aisle.

There's a tightness in my chest when I think of her. I run a hand over my white shirt, willing the pain to subside.

"You okay?" Rhea asks me. A smile is still plastered on her gloss coated lips as she talks to me and puts on a show for our guests. Elena seated us at a sweetheart table at the front of the reception hall while the rest of our wedding party was scattered around with their families. At first, I didn't have a clue what a sweetheart table meant, but now I enjoy having a moment with just Rhea and not a slew of people surrounding me. Even if they're all still watching us.

"Just thinking," I tell her, cutting into the steak on my plate.

"About?" She asks, flashing me a sweet smile as she brings a bite of baked ziti to her lips.

I purse my lips, wanting to keep this piece of myself under wrap, but her green eyes look to me expectantly. This woman is my wife and I can't even share a simple piece of information with her.

"My mother," I say hesitantly.

Rhea's eyes flash with remorse. "I understand," she tells me. Her hand moves to the cross that hangs from her neck, rubbing over the worn gold surface. "It's hard not having them here."

I feel like an asshole for forgetting that her mom is also dead. "I'm sorry," I murmur.

"It's fine," She shrugs.

"Hey," I grab her hand, bringing it into my palm and running my fingers over the surface. "I'm sorry she's not here. I wish I could change that for you."

Tears pool at the lower lash line of her green irises. Her lips part slightly, readying to say something, but she doesn't get the chance before the chiming of forks against wine glasses fills the room.

"Kiss!" Someone calls, one of my aunts, I think. Rhea is still staring at me, still looking mournful as I press my lips to hers. Our third kiss ever. I don't kiss her lightly, instead wrapping an arm around her to bring her closer to me and take my time kissing her, not caring if I'm putting on a show for the large audience before us.

When I pull away her eyes find mine and for a moment the rest of the room melts away, leaving just the two of us here. For the first time since I met her, she looks vulnerable sitting before me.

I want to erase all of her pain, dissolve all the memories that weigh on her, all the shame and guilt her father has placed on her. I want to take it all away and make her whole again.

She leans in for the next kiss and I realize this is the first time she's made a move on me. Her soft lips find mine for a gentle, lingering kiss. Her citrus and honey scent intoxicates me, and I only want more of her lips on mine. I'm addicted to the feeling. Relishing the taste.

My hand finds her face, grazing against the smooth skin of her cheek. When I pull back again, I can hear the cheering of the guests around us and a pink heat rushes to Rhea's cheeks.

"Embarrassed?" I ask with a smile. "Ya know," I tell her when she doesn't respond. "Everyone out there is jealous of you."

Her eyes roll and she gives me a serious look. "Gian…"

"I'm serious, *cara*. Every single person in this room, hell outside of this room, wishes they could be in the position that you're in."

"Close to you?" Her eyebrows lift with the question.

My lips twitch into a smirk. "Exactly."

"Self-obsessed much?"

A deep chuckle leaves my lips. "Oh, *cara mia,* you'll soon realize that I am worth the obsession."

My bride acts like the perfect wife as she dances, holding onto the tiny fingers of my niece. She smiles pleasantly and hugs each one of our relatives.

If you didn't know better, you'd think she wanted to be here.

Gio brings me man after man who wants to request a favor from me. We sit in the back corner of the venue, the area swept for bugs, and Gio keeps prying ears away.

"One last meeting," Gio tells me as the last man leaves the table.

I sigh heavily. "Thank God."

The heels attached to my little sister's feet click loudly as she walks to the table and sits down across from me. A small grin spreads on Gio's lips and he raises a hand to try to hide it.

"This is my meeting?" I ask, taking in my sister. She wears her pale pink matron of honor dress with her hair twisted back into a low bun.

"She says you promised her a favor and she'd like to collect." Gio shrugs. "Wouldn't take no for an answer."

"Alright then, tell me what you want so I can take my bride and leave," I tell Gemma.

My sister smiles brightly and my stomach rolls thinking about what she could possibly want. Something for her husband's business, surely. My sister is a smart woman, but her heart is always in the wrong place, always advocating for others instead of herself.

She'll likely ask me for some sort of deal to help Liam's dealings. Something that will piss me off to no end, but I did this to myself. I let her bank a favor and now she's here to claim.

"I want you to be nice to Rhea."

Gio and I both still at her request.

"What?" I ask, not even sure what she means. Be nice to my wife? "Why would I not be nice to my wife?"

A single eyebrow raises as she regards me. "You know how you can be, G. You're not kind. You're manipulative, you're cocky, you're demanding, I could go on and on."

"Please don't," I interrupt.

"All of those things make you good at what you do," she says and I think that's the first compliment my sister has ever given me. "But you forget where the line is. You forget to turn off that part of your personality when you get home. I'm asking that you try, just try to turn that off and be kinder to Rhea. She didn't ask for this, she didn't want to be a boss's wife and yet here she is.

The least you can do is make her happy while she plays the part of your wife."

I think over her words for a minute. She's not wrong. I am an asshole, it's ingrained in my personality, has been for a long time. She wants me to change myself for Rhea's comfort, be kinder to the woman I forced to marry me.

"That's your favor?" I ask. "That's really what you want to redeem?"

"Yes," she says without hesitation. "That's what I'm asking for."

I think I underestimated my sister, just a little. I wasn't wrong when I thought she'd redeem her favor for someone else's gain, but I truly thought it would be for her Irish husband and not for my wife.

"Fine," I tell her. "Consider it done."

She rises from her seat with a smile stretched across her lips. "Thank you," she says, pressing a quick kiss to my cheek. "And congratulations."

***

"You were gone a while," Rhea says simply as we enter the hotel suite booked for us. We were just going to be here one night. I had no plans for us to take a honeymoon until I had my city under control and my bride didn't seem to mind. She never even asked if I wanted one or why we weren't having one.

Though, if I had to guess, she had little interest in going away with me.

"Work," I tell her.

"On our wedding night?" A soft smile rises on her face while she admonishes me.

I hold my hand to my chest, feigning hurt. "Are you, the queen of sass, teasing me?"

Her eyes roll at the comment. "I'm not that sassy," she says.

I can't help but to laugh. Rhea is the sassiest person I've met, even worse than my younger sister. I slide my suit jacket off my shoulders, tossing it over the chair and sending my bow tie with it. I loosen the top few buttons of my shirt before rolling the sleeves and looking around the room for alcohol.

"You're being dramatic," she adds.

I make my way over to the minibar, finding a bottle of champagne sitting on ice just waiting for us. I take my time popping the cork and pouring two glasses while Rhea watches my every move.

"To us," I say, handing her a matching flute filled with the bubbly liquid.

"To us," she repeats, clinking her glass against mine before bringing it to her lips.

It's a good bottle, something expensive left for us by the hotel staff. Even with the price tag, it's not quite my type of drink. I'd much prefer a glass of whiskey or cognac.

Rhea downs the glass, letting the sparkling wine burn its way down her throat.

"Easy there," I tell her, earning myself a pointed look.

She flips her dark hair over her shoulder and turns her back to me. "Can you help me?" she asks.

I take my time walking to her, before tracing my fingers over the delicate skin of her back, down to the curve of her waist. Her dress is perfect for her. Subtly sexy, it's sophisticated while also showing off her figure.

"I don't think I ever told you how much I appreciate this dress," I tell her.

She peers over her shoulder at me through a veil of dark curls. "I didn't pick it for you."

"And yet, I like it."

A sly smile grows on her cheeks that she tries to suppress. "Are you going to unzip it?" she asks.

Slowly, I bring my fingers to the side of the dress where her zipper rests. I slide the zipper down and Rhea does the rest, slipping her arms through the sleeves and letting the silk fabric tumble to the floor in a heap.

She steps out of her dress, leaving it there on the floor. A pair of strappy heels are still covering her feet and she stands in front of me in nothing but the shoes and a lacy white matching corset and thong.

Her smooth tanned skin glows in the dim light of the room and the white undergarments make her seem innocent, even though the look on her face tells me she's not.

"So," she whispers.

She's acting demure, but the confidence radiates from her.

The way she carries herself, even standing half-clothed before me, is stunning.

I feel myself stiffen beneath my trousers and I have the urge to weave my fingers through her hair.

"So," I repeat, wanting her to explicitly tell me what she wants. I don't want to move in and make her hate me more. I don't want to push myself on her if this isn't what she wants. I'm not that much of an asshole, I won't force her.

But if she continues to stand in front of me dressed like that, I won't have much of a choice.

"We're married now," she whispers.

"Rhea, you're gonna have to say it because if you continue to stand there with that fucking look in your eyes, I won't be able to control myself."

A sly smile slowly grows on her lips. "I wasn't sure you'd give me a choice," she says. "I thought you were the type of man who takes what he wants."

"Is that an invitation?" I ask.

"Maybe."

I groan. This woman is damn frustrating. "I need you to say it, *cara.*"

She takes her time, a sensual smirk playing on her lips as she lets her hands run over her abdomen, finding their way to her tits. "Fuck me, Gian," she finally breathes, unleashing the monster inside me.

I step closer to her, pulling her into my grasp with urgency.

She's ignited a fire in me, bringing forth an unhinged part of me.

"Do you need it gentle?" I ask, bringing my mouth to the nape of her neck and nipping her skin softly.

"Don't be soft with me," She demands. "I want it rough."

The words feel like a permission slip to take what I want. I fist the dark curls in my hand, pulling her neck taut and forcing her to look up at me. "Are you sure, *cara?* Do you know what you're asking for?"

"Yes," she breathes.

"I won't be gentle with you."

"Stop talking, Gian, and fuck me."

My lips twist up into a smirk. "As you wish."

I lead her step-by-step back to the bed and for the first time since I've known her, she goes willingly.

Her lips are twisted just slightly, a sly smile spreading on them.

I paint this picture of her in my mind.

Her tanned skin, the way her dark hair falls over her shoulders, her ample cleavage spilling over the edge of the white lace. I'm addicted to this image of her, I want it seared in my mind until this picture is synonymous with her name.

When the backs of her thighs hit the edge of the mattress, I give her a light push, letting her fall back onto the cushion, catching herself with the palms of her hands. Doe eyes peer up at me through thick lashes as she waits quietly.

I bring my hands to the mattress, feeling it dip as I crawl over her, sliding my body over the length of her before I reach her face. I bring one hand to cup her cheek as I kiss her deeply, the last gentle kiss before I devour her, taking her bottom lip between my teeth and nipping gently.

My hands explore her body, taking in every inch of her smooth skin, relishing the feeling of it as I glide my finger over her collarbone. Goosebumps rise on her flesh as I continue my explorations and her emerald eyes squeeze shut.

"Open your eyes, baby girl," I warn her. "I want you to see who's touching you, who's fucking you, who's making you shake and cry until you come."

Her breath hitches, catching in the back of her throat as her pretty little mouth pops open.

"That's right, baby," I tell her. "I'm going to fuck you so hard until you see stars in the back of your eyes and your pretty little throat is raw from screaming my name."

"You're awfully cocky," she purrs, her claws coming out and scratching down the skin of my back.

"Shh, baby girl. I don't want to hear you speak unless you're calling me daddy? Do you understand me?"

"Yes, daddy." The corner of her lips pop up into a mischievous smirk.

My hand wraps around the curve of her ass as I give her a punishing squeeze. "Don't sass me, baby," I tell her as I continue working my way down her body with a torturously slow touch.

A low moan leaves her lips, her back arching under my touch.

I find my way to the slit of her pussy, only covered with a small scrap of fabric that I easily push aside.

"You're wet for me," I tell her with a smug smile. "You talk such a big game, baby girl, but you melt under my touch, literally dripping for me."

"Shut up, Gian," she growls.

A throaty chuckle escapes my throat. "Nah, baby. I think I'm going to keep telling you what a naughty little girl you are. I think your pussy loves it when I talk to you like this, hmm? Is that right?" I slip a finger through her folds as I say the words, feeling her body quiver under my touch.

"Ahh," I coo, hearing her whimper. I trace my finger over her clit, drawing small lazy circles with the wetness I've gathered there. Her hips twitch and I can see her body clench beneath my touch.

"Fuck," she moans, her breathing deepened and ragged.

"That's right," I tell her, "Be a good girl and let me play with your pussy."

She trembles beneath me as I drag my finger lower, finding her entrance and sliding a single digit in. My thumb drifts to her clit, continuing my assault on her tight bud of nerves. She squirms under my touch and her breathing comes out in uneven pants.

"I'm gonna come," she moans as my fingers caress her. Her head flies back and her back arches as she rides the waves of her orgasm, moans escaping her lips as she succumbs to the pleasure.

Before she's even finally come down, I flip her onto her

stomach, finding the ties of her corset and tugging swiftly to unravel the thing. Her eyes are dazed when I flip her back over, releasing her tits from the contraption.

This is the most peaceful I've ever seen the woman, the happiest she's ever looked.

"Don't pass out on me yet," I whisper. "I still have so much planned for you."

I lean back, rising from the bed so I can unbuckle and remove my pants. Rhea's hazy, blissed out gaze stays trained on me as I strip off my shirt and finally my boxers, releasing my cock.

Her tongue darts across her lips at the sight of my member and I take my time crawling back onto her, drawing out the moment and making her shiver in anticipation.

"Gian," she mewls as I slide myself into her, letting her body adjust itself to my size.

"That's right, baby, say my name." It's not long until I'm thrusting into her, balls deep. Feeling her shake with each meeting of our hips.

Soft moans and panting escape from her lips, creating a melody around us, the sounds making me harder than I thought possible.

She's so fucking beautiful when her eyes squeeze shut, her mouth popping open, unable to contain the pleasure rocking her body. I love the faces she makes, the sounds that leave her, the feeling of her skin, soft and subtle beneath me.

I feel myself tensing, my body closer to release. It takes effort to drag my cock from her, letting myself spill onto her stomach in long ropes of cum.

"Fuck," I breathe, my head coming out of the haze of sex.

Rhea pants beneath me, her body covered in a sheen of sweat and cum. She looks stunning like this, even more beautiful than she was with the corset or wedding dress.

This is my favorite look on her, satiated and covered in my cum.

Chapter Thirteen

RHEA

I'm still in a sex-induced haze when I open my eyes. I can't remember the last time I've been fucked like that, until my eyes roll back and stars dance around in my head. My body feels weak, my mouth dry.

I had no intentions of fucking Gian. I planned to lure him into a sexless marriage, make him regret forcing me into this arrangement. But then I talked to Gemma and he was vulnerable about his mother. Not to mention he looked like sin in his wedding suit, his dark hair slicked back and that devilish smile dancing on his lips.

Even after he disappeared for half the reception, giving me a preview to my life as a mafia wife, I still wanted him. I wanted to feel his body pressed against mine, his fingers between my legs. I wanted every inch of what Gian DelGado had to give—and it was delicious.

God, the dirty words that left his mouth had left me blushing. I couldn't stand him, despised his cockiness, but if he continued to make me come like that he might make a mob wife out of me sooner than later.

The other side of the bed is cold and empty when I open my eyes and roll over. I bring myself to a seated position, my eyes scanning the room, looking for my new husband. I come up empty.

"Gian?" I ask into the abyss.

He emerges from the bathroom, adjusting the cuffs of his white silk button down, his eyebrows raising in a questioning look.

"I just didn't know where you went," I whisper, as if I need an excuse for why I was looking for him.

"Missing me already?" he asks with a sly smirk.

I huff, tossing the fluffy comforter off my body, exposing my naked form wearing only a tiny white lace thong. Gian's eyes rake over my body, taking in everything he had last night.

I expect him to come over and touch me, to whisper to me that I'm beautiful like he did last night. Or to even acknowledge what happened between these sheets less than eight hours ago.

But he doesn't. Instead, he pivots on the heels of his loafers and heads to the mirror. "We need to go soon," he says, his eyes not even coming back to look at me. "I'll take you to the house first before I have to go."

A pang of disappointment strikes my chest. I'm not sure why. I haven't been reserved about me not wanting this marriage. It's not a secret that I didn't want to be stuck with Gian. But when he tells me he's not spending our first day married together, sadness flows over me.

He couldn't take more than one day off for our wedding? Not to mention it's Sunday. Why is he even working today?

"It's Sunday," I say.

A rough chuckle leaves his mouth. "Ah, nagging already, Rhea?"

The question makes anger burn in my chest. I wouldn't call my statement nagging, it was simply an observation of the day.

"I was under the impression you had no interest in spending time with me." He finally pivots his body to face me again before taking slow steps over to where I'm sitting on the bed. "If you want me to cancel my plans and spend the day with you, all you have to do is ask, Rhea."

I tug my bottom lip between my teeth. I don't want to admit my disappointment, show him a chip in my armor. "No," I say. "You don't need to cancel anything. I'm happy on my own."

"Okay," he laughs. "Get ready then."

Gian is sitting next to me on the cream leather seats of his Escalade, or someone's Escalade. Before today, I didn't know he had an Escalade, until we stepped out of the hotel and one of his men was leaning against the passenger door waiting for us.

It felt weird being driven around, like some kind of royalty. I chuckle to myself at the thought. Fucking mafia royalty, that's what I am now.

"Why are you laughing?" he asks, not bothering to look up from the black iPhone his eyes are glued to.

"Nothing, just suddenly realizing what I've gotten myself into."

His eyes lift at that, glancing over to make sure I'm still sane. "Do you have regrets?" he asks, which only serves to make me laugh harder.

"I think I would have needed the option of a choice in order for me to have regrets."

Gian takes a turn to chuckle now. "Will I hear about that for the rest of my life?"

"Probably," I smirk.

The Escalade slows down and pulls into a long driveway that spirals up a hill leading up to a beautiful white stone mansion. The house looks huge, much larger than it did in the pictures Gian handed me in his office a few weeks ago.

I didn't end up picking a house. He didn't ask again after I left his office, and I didn't bring it back up. I assumed he picked whichever one he wanted.

His choice was excellent, just too big. Though every house in that folder was this size. I liked the little condo he took me to after our engagement party. It was smaller and modern. This thing in front of me feels like a castle.

I didn't want to live in a mansion. I have no desire to plan parties and be the envy of all our neighbors. I would much prefer an apartment or a little townhouse. Why did we need something so… *lavish?*

"This is… too much."

"Then you should have picked." Gian says coolly as he exits the car, sliding his cell phone into his pocket. "I have business to attend to," he says walking around the car to stand next to me. "Andrew here will take you anywhere you need to go. The house is decorated and it should have all the essentials. Your boxes from Joe's will arrive this afternoon and if you need anything else, just ask Andrew." He spouts off the information while dropping a key into my hand. "Anything else?" His eyebrows lift expectantly.

"My car is at my father's house."

"I sold that." The statement leaves his lips with no emotion. "Andrew will drive you."

My fists clench. Why would he just sell my car without consulting me? "Gian," I try to inhale, try to calm myself so I don't lash out at this man. For a second, I was starting to like him or at least not hate him. But so quickly he reminded me of the kind of man that he is. The type of man that thinks he can control me, walk into my life and make decisions without even consulting me. I feel stupid for forgetting who I was dealing with. For momentarily letting my guard down.

"Gi—"

"Don't argue with me." He waves his hand dismissively. "It's already done. You don't need it, it's sold. Find something more interesting to argue about, *cara.*"

Red tints the edges of my vision. "You're an asshole," I snap.

"Mm-hmm." He smirks. "So I've been told." He gives me a sly nod and then heads to his BMW conveniently parked in our new driveway. So he gets a car and I don't? Seems like there's a sick double standard going on in this house.

One day of marriage and I already want to grab the car keys from Andrew and ram the Escalade into my husband's body as hard as possible.

I march into the house to prevent myself from committing a murder in broad daylight. Using my brand new key I let myself into the mansion. At least whoever he hired to decorate the place had fantastic taste.

There's a beautiful open living space looking out into the large kitchen. The dark hardwood floors stretch across the house, covering all the floors my eyes can see from here. The walls are painted a soothing cream color and the room is filled with neutral furnishing and small touches of gold and brass. The place feels cozy and I want to collapse on the large cream sofa and just melt away.

What is a mob wife supposed to do, anyway?

Any other Sunday I'd be crawling out of bed around this time and sitting at my desk with my laptop, working on cases or studying for my bar exam.

I don't even know where to go in this house to work. Everything is so clean and pretty, I barely want to touch it. Plus, my law books are packed away waiting to be moved from my old room at my father's house to this one.

I wonder what Elena is doing or how the house feels without me and Christopher there. How will she survive being alone with my father? I cringe at the thought. I don't know how she does it.

I wander toward the kitchen, taking in the white cupboards and tile backsplash. There's a large farmhouse sink sitting in front of the window and a set of double ovens that gleam under the kitchen light. I run my hands over the marble countertops, feeling the sleek surface under my palm.

The urge to cook suddenly overtakes me. Cooking has been my safe haven since I was a kid. My mother taught me how to cook in the tiny apartment kitchen. We were dirt poor and ate far too much pasta, but my mother could turn any meal into something gourmet.

I open the sleek double door fridge to find it filled. Only my husband would have a fully stocked kitchen for a wife he barely knows. I shake the thought of how privileged the man is as I pull ricotta and parmesan from the fridge. In the pantry I find a box of ziti noodles and cans of tomatoes and paste. I grab a few of everything, bringing it back out to the counter.

I start by simmering the garlic in oil as I open all the cans of tomatoes. Chopping an onion from the pantry, I add a handful of small pieces to the pan, letting them get fragrant in the oil.

Cooking has a rhythm, an art to it. My mother always taught me to feel the emotion of the dish when cooking. I listen to my ingredients, learn what they like and what pairs well with them.

The onion and garlic have cooked, the white of the onion turning translucent in the pot's bottom. I add the tomato paste, stirring it swiftly into the combination of garlic and onion before deglazing it with a red wine. I bring the bottle to my lips after adding a splash to the pan.

Wine for the sauce, wine for me. Only fair, right?

I add in my tomatoes, smashing them into smaller pieces, and let the whole thing stew on a low temperature. I love making sauce, it was the first thing my mom taught me. "There's no recipe," she would tell me as we dumped the contents of tomato cans into the large cooking pot. "You just have to *feel* it," she'd tell me. "Cook with your heart, not your brain, *cuore mia.*"

When I moved in with my dad and Elena I wanted nothing to do with them, I had no desire to be a part of a new family. It pissed my father off to no end. He wanted me to 'just get over it.' Elena didn't pressure me.

I had a picture of stepmoms built up in my head. I had the idea that they were mean, vile creatures who hated their stepchildren. By all accounts, Elena had every reason to hate me. I was the daughter of her husband's mistress, conceived while she was home with a newborn. But Elena never held it against me.

I learned even more about cooking from her. Fusing her Sicilian style with my mother's Northern Italian style, I was practically a professional at Italian cooking. Elena had hoped I'd become a chef or go to cooking school, but this was my passion not a profession. I didn't want to blur my love for food with the

142

job that brought home money. I never wanted to hate cooking, and in most cases doing what you love for money only makes you bitter.

Filling a pot with water, I bring it over to the stove, turning it on to boil. I'll parcook the ziti while the sauce cooks, getting it ready to be baked. I barely have the pot on the stove when I hear it. A loud banging sound outside. The deafening impact makes me drop to my knees, spilling the water over the hardwood. I bring my hands to my ears, offering little protection to them.

I have the urge to stand back up, to chase down the sound, but my heart is racing and my body is paralyzed and unable to move from sheer fear.

Right when I think I can breathe again, I hear the front door swing open.

Chapter Fourteen

GIAN

Rhea's pussy is the only thing on my mind today. It's preventing me from listening to the men in my office, from hearing about their dealings and offering my advice. Too much of my job lately is listening.

I'm good at it. I was trained to listen to the things not said, to the messages hidden between every line. It makes me better at helping them, better at seeing the possibilities, knowing the consequences of every action.

Rafi swings the door open to my office at Alibi. I choose to meet with men here, it's bigger than the office at the pizza shop and nicer. We used to sit around the tables at the restaurant to do business, but now with more issues and the chance of someone eavesdropping, we opt for the club instead.

His face is frantic when he looks at me, which maybe explains why he didn't knock and rushed in instead. I let my irritability at the intrusion slide.

"Boss," he says, the tone of his voice too high. "They attacked."

"Who?" I ask. Any attack is serious, but the urgency in his words makes me think the hit must have been on Gio or taken out a whole gang of men.

"Your house," he says, "They almost got to Rhea."

My heart stops, a numbness creeping over me. "Who?" I ask again, acknowledging that Rafi didn't actually answer my question. "Who the fuck was it?" I demand, rising from the chair and whipping down the newspaper I'd been holding, smacking the rolled bundle against my desk.

For the first time I see Rafi shake, fear radiates off him from my yelling. "I don't know," his eyes lower as he says the words.

He doesn't know? How does he not know? Why would he barge in here with a problem and no answers?

"Find out," I growl. "We're done here," I say to the men sitting in my office. "I want to know who just attacked me," I tell them, grabbing my suit jacket from the back of the chair and sliding it up my arms.

"Where are you going?" Gio asks.

"To see my wife."

Rhea is huddled in the bedroom when I get there. Her knees are tucked to her chest and all the lights are off with the curtains drawn. She sits on the floor beside the bed, far from all the windows that look out into our backyard.

I stand in the doorway, taking her in for a moment. "Are you okay?"

Her head snaps up, her emerald eyes meeting mine. She hops to her feet, coming toward me at a quick pace. I think she's going to hit me, slap me or scream at me for getting her into this situation, but instead she wraps her arms around me, pressing her face into my shirt.

I let my arms circle around her, running a hand over her back in a soothing motion. "I'm sorry, *cara mia*," I whisper. "I'm sorry this happened."

She pulls back just enough to show me her glossy eyes. "What *did* happen?" she asks.

I scrub a hand over my face, keeping her secured against me with the other. "I have men finding out," I tell her.

I feel terrible that this was her first day as my wife. Alone and attacked. I told her I would protect her, keep her safe, and now she's no safer with me than she was with Joe. "Is this what it's going to be like?" she asks, her voice soft and filled with fear.

This was the reason I didn't want a wife in the first place. I didn't want someone close to me that would be made vulnerable because of her proximity to me. I thought a fake marriage would be easier, that I wouldn't care if anything happened to her.

But looking down at Rhea, her glassy emerald eyes searching for answers, I realize I was wrong. I do care. I will hunt down whoever tried to hurt her and gut them.

No one touches my family.

Rhea included.

"Why does the house smell so good?" I ask, prompting her to lift her face from its place currently pressed against my chest.

"I cooked," she says.

"You cooked?" Her statement shocks me. The woman had been so determined not to do a single wifely thing since I met her. Didn't plan the wedding, didn't pick the house, I assumed she didn't cook either.

She points her head in the direction of the kitchen. "It should be done."

I follow her downstairs to the large kitchen. I dismiss Andrew from watching over Rhea inside, but have him stay close by. I have a few other enforcers outside watching over the place, wanting as many eyes as possible on the house in case someone comes back to finish the job.

By Andrew's account, a black car drove by, slowing down to fire off a few shots before racing away. He got a partial plate number that I didn't think would get us anywhere without more information. Apparently after the botched hit when Andrew came in to check on Rhea she freaked out, thinking it was someone coming to get her.

She swung a pan at his head.

I chuckled when he told me that part. Luckily for him, she missed. But that was something we'd need to work on, because the next time she's attacked, I don't want her to knock him out.

Rhea covers her hands with pot holders and pulls a casserole dish from the oven. "Baked ziti," she tells me.

It smells delicious, I catch a waft of the basil as she sets the pan on the stove. It reminds me of my mother's cooking, drool pooling in my mouth at the thought. I haven't had a homemade meal for almost two years now.

The woman loved to cook. She was the type of mother who always had a plate of cookies sitting out when I got home from school. She cooked homemade sauce that simmered on the stove for hours every Sunday, filling the house with the scent of basil, garlic, and tomatoes.

The smell of Rhea's food gives me the feeling of home, the warmth of good memories slipping over me like a warm embrace.

Rhea searches the cabinets for plates until she finds them, pulling out two and filling each with a portion of her baked ziti. I grab napkins and silverware and join her at the table.

"This feels like a fucked up first dinner in our house," she says as she slides into the chair across from me.

I chuckle, "Yeah, it does." Her ziti looks perfect, the ricotta mixture spread through evenly with a generous layer of sauce on top. I bring a forkful to my mouth, groaning as the flavors explode on my taste buds. I let my eyes roll back into my head, enjoying the moment of her food on my tongue.

"This is amazing," I tell her.

A smile lights up her features. It's much more genuine than

the one plastered to her lips yesterday. Her wedding smile was fake, a façade put on to appease me. But this one is real.

"Thank you," she says, her delicate fingers lifting to graze over the cross that dangles from her neck.

"What do you think about when you do that?" I ask, pointing my fork in the direction of the charm.

Her eyes snap to meet mine and she drops the charm from her fingertips quickly. "Nothing," she says, stabbing a noodle with her fork.

"Tell me," I say, the words coming out harsher than I intended. I'm too accustomed to making demands. Being soft and gentle isn't something I'm sure I even know how to do anymore. "Please," I add.

Green eyes stare at me for a moment. "My mother," she whispers, her eyes dropping to avoid my gaze.

I nod my head, understanding flooding over me. "She taught you how to cook?" I ask.

"Yeah." She smiles softly.

"Was it hard, moving in with Joe after her death?"

Her eyes scan me again. We never talked about what happened to her mother, but she doesn't seem surprised that I know.

She laughs low. "It was terrible."

I can't help but smile at her words. I can't begin to imagine what that house must have been like growing up.

"Tell me something happy then," I say, wanting to bring that smile back to her face. I want to see her light up again, I want an emotion out of her that's not sadness or hatred.

She smiles shyly as she looks to me, biting her lip softly before answering. "I have this fantasy," she starts. "That I pass my bar exam, open my own office, and help people. The people that the government and the law refuse to help. That my job, that my life means something." She closes her eyes as she speaks. The vulnerability of her words isn't lost on me.

I stand up, dusting off my suit pants and walking to her side of the table. I extend a hand for her to take as she stands up in front of me. I wrap her in my arms again, bringing her close to me as I whisper in her ear. "That's not a fantasy," I tell her. "You can have that."

She tilts her head back to look up to me. She feels small in my embrace, different from the strong woman I encountered that first day at my father's office. But I like her like this. I like both versions of her. The strong take no shit version and the one that's comfortable enough to be vulnerable with me.

Slowly, she rises to her tiptoes and brings her lips to me, kissing me soft and gentle.

"I don't think I'm hungry anymore," I whisper on her lips.

"Me either." Her breath hitches when she responds, coming out in a throaty sound.

I take my hands from her only long enough to push the plates back to the other side of the table, making room for me to lie Rhea back on the long wooden surface. Raking my hands over her stunning body, I move down to the hem of her leggings, sliding the black material down over her hips. Her pussy is bare underneath, not a scrap of fabric keeping me from her slick heat.

"Fuck," I practically growl. "Your pussy looks fucking delicious, baby girl."

Red heat rises to her cheeks, the color spreading down over her collarbone. She brings a hand to her mouth, as if she can hide her embarrassment by covering her lips and muffling all of her sounds.

"Uncover you mouth, baby," I tell her. "I want to hear every sound you make. I want to hear every moan, every fucking whimper."

When she doesn't move, I bring my mouth down to her mound, flicking my tongue over her pussy lips. "If you don't listen, I will pin your hands down and whisper every little dirty thing I want to do to you into your pretty little ears until you're a fucking puddle beneath me."

Slowly, her hand slips off her mouth and glides down to grip the wood beneath her.

"Good girl," I coo, bringing my mouth back down to her pussy. I push a hand against her thigh, forcing her to spread herself wider for me, making room for me to dive into her sweet cunt.

I drag my finger through her wet slit, spreading her wetness up to her clit. She shivers beneath me and chuckles softly. I've barely touched her. If she is this sensitive already I can only imagine how she'll be screaming once I get my tongue on her clit.

I take my time, using a finger to thrust into her entrance,

opening her up for me.

"That's it, baby," I tell her, finger fucking her until she's shaking. Then, I add the second finger, curling them so they pound into her g-spot. I bring my mouth to her wet heat, licking along her seam until I find her clit. I draw circles with my tongue, lapping up her wetness.

She's moaning, writhing beneath me as soft sounds escape her lips. It's a fucking beautiful melody, one I never want to stop, but I can feel her body getting closer. Her pussy grips around my fingers, bringing my cock to life. I can't wait to have myself buried in her pussy.

"Are you close, sweet girl?" I ask her, not easing the thrust of my fingers and only removing my mouth from her clit long enough to ask the question.

"Yes," she breathes and I can hear the need in her voice, dripping from the word.

"Come for me," I demand. "Come for me, Rhea." I pull her clit beneath my lips, sucking the tight bundle of nerves. Rhea complies, crashing over the edge of her orgasm with quick pants and shaking legs. Her breathing is uneven as she finally cascades over the edge, shaking the remnants of her release.

"Fuck," she moans.

I grab her hips, pulling her down until her pussy hits the end of the table.

"That was too intense," she whines. "Gian, I can't take anymore."

A smirk rises on my lips as I bring the two fingers that were just stuffed in her cunt to the seal of my lips, sliding them into my mouth and licking the taste of her from them. Her emerald eyes are fixated on me as I do so. I moan when I remove the fingers, sucking the last taste of her from my skin. "I fucking love the taste of you, Rhea," I tell her. "So fucking sweet for me."

A noise somewhere between a growl and a moan escapes her lips as I unzip my pants, dropping them to the floor along with my boxers.

My cock is hard and aching for a taste of her sweet pussy. Her cunt is dripping for me as I line the head with her wet heat, sliding myself into her. Her moans meet my thrusts as we find a pace mending our bodies together.

She feels like pure bliss beneath me.

I lean my body forward, capturing one her tits in my hand and palming it roughly through her shirt. Her nipple perks up for me, straining through the fabric of her shirt. I lift her shirt, exposing her flesh so I can bring my mouth to her nipple, dragging the bud between my teeth.

She's panting again, her breathing rapid. I can feel her pussy gripping my cock, ready to milk me as she comes undone.

"Who's pussy is this?" I ask, bringing down a slap onto her sensitive flesh.

"Yours," she moans, shifting her hips against me for more friction, meeting each of my thrusts.

"Tell me, baby, who's cock is fucking you right now?"

"Yours," she cries. "Your cock, Gian."

With the last words she comes undone around me, her pussy gripping my dick and milking me dry. I fall over her, leaning into my arms as I pant through the aftershocks of my orgasm. "Fuck," I moan.

"Fuck," Rhea repeats.

Chapter Fifteen

RHEA

"Are you even listening?" Gemma asks me, her heel tapping furiously on the floor of my office. My head snaps up, dropping the pen that had been mindlessly spinning between my fingers. My eyes find her heart-shaped face scowling at me. Both hands are poised on her hips as she waits for my response.

"Sorry," I mutter. My head has been out of the game for weeks now. Marriage to Gian is fucking with me. He's never home, leaving me to return to an empty house guarded by far too many men, all of whom are directed not to speak to me.

It's like living in isolation, guarded like a prisoner. My anxiety has skyrocketed. My head has a constant stream of the worst case scenarios playing on a loop. Shooters, kidnappers, burglars. My mind has run rampant with the ideas of my future.

Andrew drives me around, spending his days posted in the lobby of Giuseppe's law firm with a blank stare on his face. He's my age, but he calls me *ma'am*. The word grates on my nerves, but no matter how many times I tell him to stop it, he can't shake the manners.

"You're not yourself," Gemma says, her face turning from aggressive to concerned in the matter of seconds. "What's going on?" she asks. "Is it my brother?" She adds the question in a whisper, looking out of my office to make sure Andrew isn't paying attention, which he always is. The kid has super hearing. I swear he knows my every want and need. He watches me like a hawk and reports back to my husband with such quickness.

I'll say something silly, a quip about his lack of appearances and suddenly Gian is walking through the door, as if someone had clued him into my statement. I'm certain that it's Andrew. His constant stalking has me on edge, biting my tongue and watching everything I say around him.

"No," I tell Gemma. "I don't know," I admit, dragging my fingers through my curls, stretching them as I go. Tugging on my hair has been my go-to move when I'm overwhelmed, something I've done since childhood. My mother hated it when I tugged at my natural curls. She would always swat my hand and tell me not to ruin my hair. Thinking of her, I pull my hand away quickly.

'I don't know' is the truth though. I have no idea what's wrong with me, what's throwing me off.

I don't love Gian.

I know that, so I shouldn't be bothered that he's not home. I shouldn't care when I'm eating dinner alone at night or going to bed without his body curled beneath the sheets.

He fucked me twice and you would think that I've become obsessed. Dick-whipped. Waiting for him to come home at night and wrap his arms around me.

I don't love him.

So why am I waiting up for him at night? I keep a novel gripped in my hands, waiting up under the guise that I'm reading. Some nights I'll even sit at the kitchen table with my law books, trying to study.

But it's all a ruse, even I realize that.

I'm waiting for him.

For the life of me I can't understand myself, can't comprehend my own feelings.

Gemma sighs heavily as she slumps into the chair across from my desk. "Listen," she says. "This has been a lot and it's all happened so fast. I wouldn't blame you if you weren't okay." Her dark eyes fill with sympathy, but all I can think of is how they match her brothers, the brown so dark and deep. "If you're overwhelmed, I get that." She finishes and I realize that once again I've missed half of what she was saying.

"No," I shake my shoulders, letting the tension drip from me. "I'm here," I say. "I need to get my shit together."

Her dark eyes look skeptical, but she nods. "Okay, so Bridget

Montgomery, you remember her?"

"Yep." Bridget Montgomery, nineteen-year-old college student raped by a group of football players, eight of them to be exact. My heart breaks when I think about her.

She reported the case to the school only to be tortured by her classmates, accused of lying and trying to destroy the team, because how could she possibly have been assaulted by all of them at once.

The team has a pack mentality and even though every player was at the party, not a single one saw a thing. Her story is uncorroborated, not a single witness willing to come forward. With no evidence, her case was basically dropped to the bottom of the pile and ignored. Left to rot in the bottom of a cardboard box with her last scrap of dignity.

I finger the cross around my neck. My faith has wavered on and off since the day my mom died and my life took a sharp turn for the worse, but stories like this bring my fingers to the gold charm praying to whoever is up there to stop this violence.

"They poured whiskey down her throat." Gemma recounts solemnly, "Forced it on her until she was too drunk to remember a thing."

"She had tearing," I say, flipping through the report in front of me.

"Apparently not enough," Gemma breaths.

"She needs a real lawyer." I exhale, slapping the papers down onto my desk. "Not some second rate hack who hasn't even taken the bar exam."

Gemma gives me a disapproving look. "Stop with that negativity," she scolds. "She needs help and we can help her. Are we perfect? No. But we're better than nothing."

A sad laugh escapes my lips. "Better than nothing," I repeat.

"Better than nothing." She laughs. "Put that on a business card."

Andrew is silent while we drive from the law office back to the house. He thrums his fingers against the steering wheel in tune with the pop song that flows from the speakers.

"Can I ask you something?" I say from the back seat and watch as his body stiffens at my question.

"Yes, ma'am." I cringe at the name.

"Do you report everything I do back to him?" I study him as I ask the question, his muscles are still stiff, rigid under my scrutiny.

"I don't know what you mean," he says.

I chuckle before rephrasing my question. "Do you report everything I do back to my husband, Andrew? It's a simple question really."

He sighs heavily, the breath exhaling from his lungs in a long rush. "Yes," he states simply.

It's the answer I expected. The answer that makes sense with his actions lately and with Andrew staying close to me at all times.

"Can you ask him to come home for dinner tonight then?"

I see the tension drain from Andrew's shoulders as he nods a response. "Yes, ma'am."

I make ravioli for dinner. Kneading the dough by hand for twenty minutes. There's a sparkly white Kitchen Aid in the corner, a gift from Gian the day after the drive-by. I'm not sure if it was a 'sorry you were shot at' or a 'sorry I fucked you then left before you woke up' gift. Either way, the shiny new appliance was appreciated. With the dough hook I could have the new machine doing all the hard work for me, but there's something about kneading it by hand.

My mother and Elena both always used their hands. My mother's method was more so because we were too poor to afford a fancy machine to do the work. Elena, on the other hand, had learned from her grandmother who only had her hands to do the work.

There was a certain therapy that went along with kneading pasta. There was no recipe for this. Both of my mother's taught me by feeling. By sticking my hands in the mixture and rolling it together. I could tell if the consistency was right with my eyes closed.

I put all of my anger and feelings into the dough, letting it work out everything that has bottled itself up within me over the past week. When the twenty minute timer goes off, I bundle the dough tightly in plastic wrap and move onto the filling.

Pulling the ricotta, spinach, and ground beef from the fridge, I start to work on my mixture. Cooking down the spinach and browning the beef. Another twenty minutes and I have everything ready to assemble.

I'm still in the kitchen, my apron covered in flour, when Gian comes through the front door.

"Smells good," he says, waltzing into the kitchen with a soft smile. "I like you like this, *cara*. Domestic, in the kitchen cooking for me." He grins, popping a chunk of cheese into his mouth.

A scowl etches itself across my features. Why did I want him to come home for dinner again? It definitely wasn't to listen to his cocky mouth make quips about my domestication.

"Andrew says you wanted to see me?" he questions. "You making dinner for me?"

I roll my eyes at him, sealing the ravioli I was working on and adding it to the tray of finished ones. "You're an ass," I tell him.

"Mm-hmm." He grins. "Tell me something new, *cara.*" His smile is ever present as I ignore him, continuing to fill my pasta with the meat and cheese mixture before sealing each one with the tines of a fork.

"Ya know," he says, coming around the counter and sliding his hands along my hips. A fire lights in my core against my will. My body responds to Gian's touch, to his words. Even with all my will power, I can't stop the butterflies that tumble through my stomach at the feeling of his fingers brushing under the hem of my silk top. "I think you wanted me here to fuck you." He leans in to whisper the last part into my ear, sending a chill down my spine.

"Gian." His name leaves my lips breathier than I intend it to. It sounds like a moan of pleasure instead of the warning I was trying for.

"What, *cara mia?*" he asks, a lilt to his words. "Tell me you don't want this and I'll back off." I can feel him smile into the crook of my neck as he bites down gently on the sensitive flesh. "But you and I both know you'd be lying, baby," he whispers, his breath ghosting over my neck and I feel myself tilting my head, making more room for his exploration.

"Gian," I try again, but I don't finish.

He's not wrong, if I stopped him now I would be lying, because I love what he's doing. The feeling of his hands as they skate over my skin beneath my shirt, rising to find the cups of my bra and slipping beneath the lacy fabric.

He slips his hands back out, pulling on the ties of my apron instead and letting the fabric drop to the floor.

"Turn around," he orders me as he grips my hips and does it for me. He tugs on the hem of my shirt, lifting it over my head and discarding it with the apron.

A smug smile rises on his cheeks as he takes in the lacy bra covering my tits. "You even dressed up for me, baby," he coos. "You want me, hmm?"

Heat rises to my cheeks, coloring me with a red blush that trails down my throat.

"Answer me," he demands when I stay silent for too long.

Gian's dirty mouth has me dripping and I know when he slides down my dress pants he'll find my panties wet for him.

"Rhea," He scolds me as his hand slaps against my ass cheek. Not hard enough to cause real pain, but enough to snap me out of my haze.

"No," I say, which sounds ridiculous as I stand shirtless in front of him.

A smirk flashes across his lips as his dark eyes peer down to my nipples, the tight buds straining through the lacy fabric of my bra. A calloused hand comes to my right shoulder, slipping a finger under the strap of my bra he slides it off my shoulder before moving to the other side. I stay silent as he works, unsnapping my bra from the back and letting it drop to the floor with my other articles of clothing.

"Your body says differently," he tells me, pinching one of my pink buds between two fingers. I shiver at his touch. He's not wrong, my body is primed and ready for him, aching for his touch. "I bet if I slip my fingers between your legs you'll be dripping for me." His other hand moves slowly down to the waistband of my pants. I'm panting as his hand moves, goose bumps trailing in its wake. His fingers slip under the waistband and moves down to my pussy, feeling the wetness that has already soaked through my panties.

His grin expands, the smile reaching his eyes in a way I've never seen on him. I can't help but to admire his features, self-confidence oozes from the man. Dark eyes drill into me, monitoring every movement, taking in every inch of my body. He looks over the moon at finding me wet for him. His ego inflated a bit too much.

"You love this," he purrs. "Admit it to me, *cara*. Tell me how much you love me coming home to fuck you. How wet it makes you to be a dirty little slut for me. It's just you and me here, baby." He smiles widely. "You can admit how much you want it."

His words trail over my body like silk, the truth of them drilling into me. I'm aching to feel him inside me again. The vibrator tucked away in my nightstand has nothing on Gian DelGado. His breath coasts along my neck as he waits for me to reply.

"Hmm?" he prods, feathering light kisses over my jaw.

"Yes," I moan, leaning into his touch as he strokes me over my damp panties.

"Tell me," he demands.

"I want you to fuck me, Gian."

He flips me around quickly, pushing the top half of my body down onto the counter. My hands fly forward, grasping for something to hang onto and landing on the flour that still coats the surface of our counters. I'm still off balance when Gian rips down my pants, wasting no time.

I hear him unzip his suit pants, releasing his cock and palming it slowly.

I feel dazed, frantic in my need for him to fuck me. There's flour coating my body, making my palms slip against the marble surface. A sharp slap lands on my ass cheek and I whip my head around to find Gian's handsome face twisted into a smile.

He lines his cock up with my entrance and slides himself in. He goes in quick, only pausing once he's balls deep, letting me have a moment to adjust to his size. He fills me perfectly, stretching me in all the best ways.

"You feel so fucking good, baby girl," he moans. A hand snakes up my back, brushing over my skin and reaching forward to grab a fistful of my hair. He wraps the locks around his fist, pulling my head taut.

I'm so close, the edge of my orgasm is pricking at my skin, every inch of me is taut in anticipation. Then Gian slows, his pace comes to a crawl, leaving me hanging on the edge.

I want to scream at him to plead for release. My head drops to the counter, flour rising up at the movement, coating my skin further.

A finger comes to the tight ring above the one his dick is currently in, swirling my juices around and prodding lightly.

"Do you think you can handle this?" he asks.

Flipping my hair over my shoulder, I turn my head enough to look at him. It's a fucking gorgeous sight, not that I would admit that to him. His shirt is roughly unbuttoned, exposing the dark hair that creeps up his chest, his muscles are taut against the white fabric, his six-pack clearly on display. One hand is resting on the curve of my ass while the other threatens to breach my back entrance.

I've never had anal sex, never let anyone go where Gian wants to right now. It feels erotic to give that to him, to let him have that part of me. Adrenaline streams through my body and the sexual goddess inside of me is begging for release. "I don't know," I finally tell him.

"Let me try," he urges, swirling that finger around, so fucking close to just pressing in. "Just a finger tonight, baby."

"Yes," I moan and without hesitation he pushes through. The tension begins to build again, rising in my core and taking over all my senses. The combination of his cock in my channel and the finger in my ass pushes me closer to the edge.

"Gian." His name leaves my lips in a breathless moan.

"That's right, baby," he coos. "Come for me. Show what a slut you are for this cock."

I crash over the edge of my orgasm, a dark haze clouding my vision as the waves of pleasure roll over me. I'm screaming as I fall over the edge of my orgasm, not sure if it's his name or gods that I call out.

His pace becomes brutal, his thrusts relentless. He follows me over the cliff, crying out a soft Italian curse.

We're panting heavily as he pulls out of me, leaning his back against the counter next to me, his hand coming to rest on my spine. He brings his face down to my ear, moving a tendril of hair and whispering softly.

"Good job, baby girl."

Chapter Sixteen

GIAN

Rhea finishes the pasta, boiling the ravioli that we didn't smash or knock off the counter during our fucking session. She plates them with a light sauce and a sprinkle of parsley before setting both servings on the table.

She looks stunning in my t-shirt with nothing underneath. The bottom of her ass cheeks exposed, her nipples visible through the white cotton. I can't keep my eyes off her.

"That's not why I wanted you to come home," she says once she's seated across from me.

"Yeah?" I truly didn't know why she wanted me home. I wouldn't say I've been avoiding her since the incident, more so giving her space. The idea that those men could have hurt or killed her simply because she married me was weighing heavily on my conscience lately.

I backed her into a corner with this decision. The choice I gave her didn't need to be an ultimatum in front of her family. We could have spoken ahead of time. I could have said no to the arrangement and helped her. But I wanted her to agree to marry me, and putting her on the spot like that, doing it in front of her father assured it was a yes. I didn't want to risk that she'd say no, didn't want to leave anything up to chance.

And now she's in danger because of it.

I've built up the image of a monster. Of a man lacking emotions, only concerned for himself. But that's the image I created; the image I wanted the world to see. I'm not a monster. The idea of an innocent woman being killed simply because she was born into shitty circumstances doesn't sit well with me.

And Rhea was born into the worst circumstances.

"Have you figured out who did the drive-by?" she asks, stirring around her pasta aimlessly.

"No," I tell her, much to my dismay. No fucking leads, no idea who would try to put a hit out on me or even know where to find me. The house was just bought, I hadn't even spent a night in it yet.

A long breath blows from her lips.

I reach across the table, pulling her hand into mine. "I'll figure it out," I say, attempting to comfort her.

She nods, but doesn't verbalize a response for me. I can see the curiosity and fear dance across her eyes. I don't want her to worry about staying here. "You'll be safe." I tell her, "Andrew

170

is here and I have my men outside. No one is getting inside this house."

She doesn't give me a response, still locked in her head, probably thinking of the worst outcomes. I sigh heavily, bringing my head to my palms. Next to our meals are scattered papers and Rhea's legal pad scribbled with notes.

"What are you working on?" I ask, trying to change the subject from the drive-by torturing her thoughts.

"Oh." She notices me eyeing the papers. "This case." She shrugs.

"Tell me about it," I say, more demanding than I mean to sound.

She sighs, raising her emerald eyes to look at me sternly. "You won't care," she says matter of fact.

"Try me," I deadpan.

"Fine," she breathes. When she exhales, she tells me the story of the nineteen-year-old college student. Her eyes are glassy as she speaks, the emotion threatening to spill over. She looks defeated, I can feel the emotion dripping from her words. She truly cares for this girl and there's not a thing she can do for her.

Naïve, I think, to have such hope in the law that it would help this girl. From a young age, I've known that the law doesn't protect the innocent. It aids the guilty.

Every successful person is harboring a dirty secret. They use them as stepping stones, gaining compliance from others by holding their secrets over them. Whoever knows the most secrets wins.

Those boys will never be held accountable for their actions. No matter what Rhea does, no matter what lawyer she's able to get for this girl, she will never get justice.

I give her a pitying look and she senses it immediately. "You don't believe in this. In me," she says, her tone rising with each word.

"No," I tell her. "I don't believe in the way you're trying to seek justice."

"Yeah?" She presses her lips into a thin line. "And how would you do it then?"

I inhale deeply, thinking over her question. How would I do it? For starters, I wouldn't use the legal system. I would take justice into my own hands. I lean forward on the table, resting my elbows on the wood surface, bringing my face closer toward hers.

"I would talk to one of my men, not your father, probably Paulie. Paulie has some young guys, you see. So Paulie would hire three, maybe four of his guys. Pay 'em a little, maybe 1 K each. These guys will wait for your football players, maybe after a game, a class, something like that. They get the boys alone though, pick them off one by one. Beat the crap out of them, teach 'em a lesson." I pop another bite of pasta into my mouth. "Killing's an option if you want to pay more, but that's messier and this is still effective. I would have them beat to the brink of death, make them really pay for what they did to her, but not go far enough that they can escape their punishment."

Her emerald eyes are as wide as saucers as she looks at me.

"That's how I would do it, *bella*, but you keep working that law angle."

The smell of grease and pepperoni fills my nostrils. Working in the pizza shop feels like home. The lingering scent of spices and tomatoes reminds me of my mother's kitchen. She would cook up a storm while I sat at the breakfast table finishing homework. Memorizing useless grammar rules and times tables. I knew at a young age that school wouldn't mean much for me, that I was meant for something different. The lectures, the papers, none of it was going to matter for me.

But my mother loved it. She asked me about my day as soon as I came through the door and shed my coat and backpack. Gio hated school and it never suited him. He thought outside of the boxes, beyond the lines. He wasn't meant for the kind of structure that the American education system demanded. Gemma was too focused on boys and parties. School for her was just a social life, a flurry of events and entertainment.

If one of us was going to make our mother proud, I knew it wouldn't be them.

So I tried, pretended. I put effort into something that I knew was meaningless.

My training with the boss was far more beneficial for me. My life skills, my career, everything was wrapped up in *La Famiglia*. The time I spent in that dingy basement did more for me than any amount of time spent at school.

Ma didn't see this future for me, though. She wanted to believe her family wasn't crime ridden. That this didn't run in our bloodstream. God, did she love my father, everything about the man except for the company he chose.

At some point, the fancy cars and designer clothing meant less to her. She just wanted her children to be successful... at something legal.

I would never be someone who worked a nine-to-five job and came home for dinner. Wouldn't be the father coaching little league games. I would never be 'normal.'

But sometimes when I'm sitting here in the four walls of my office, inhaling the scent of greasy pepperoni and a blend of Italian spices I can close my eyes and imagine I'm back in that kitchen doing my homework at the breakfast table.

And for a second, I believe my mother is still alive.

This world of mine, *La Famiglia,* isn't meant for women and yet we drag them in. Force them to be a part of this it and let them suffer the consequences they didn't ask for. My mother was a bystander in this war.

And so is Rhea.

I didn't mean to grow attached to her. The thought of her safety stays on my mind more than I like. Glances at my phone for updates have become ritualistic. My worry for her gnaws at my gut, tugs at my brain, clinging onto anything within reach.

I've never felt like this before.

I've always cared for my siblings, but their safety never felt like my responsibility. If Rhea gets hurt or God forbid killed, that would be my fault. I dragged her into this marriage kicking and screaming.

Anything that happens to her is my burden.

Instead of telling her any of this, the guilt that rests on my shoulder, I've just avoided her since the day of the incident. As if avoiding her would make me feel better. The thoughts of her still play through my head like a slideshow. A constant reminder of what I've attached myself to. The gold ring on my finger shines in the sunlight, screaming 'you've dragged another life into this.'

How is it possible I could love something with my whole heart, my whole being, and still know that it's wrong? Still know that it's not something I want to force someone else into.

The bells above the door chimes as it opens. A tall figure enters the restaurant, tipping his head to Sal, who stands at the counter.

His eyes scan the small restaurant until they land on me, sitting alone in the back corner of the pizza joint. Cheap, knock-off loafers stroll across the black-and-white checkered floor toward me.

"Gian DelGado," The man says, the tone of his voice is bitter, holding on to some amount of anger.

He has thinning hair and a pale face. His skin looks dull and the suit that hangs limply from his body is cheap, and looks quite scratchy.

"You must be my new FBI agent," I state, forcing a small grin to rise on my cheeks. That means agent Baldwin was fired. One less thing to worry about. If they fired him, they probably found the evidence I planted, the fingerprints trailing through a dead man's apartment.

If this fucker was smart, he'd stay away. Do the opposite of his predecessor and avoid a life sentence. Or an early grave.

But if they were smart, they wouldn't have joined the FBI in the first place.

"What can I do for you?" I ask the guy.

Each of his hands comes to his scrawny hips, pulling back the sun bleached suit jacket and standing with some sort of false authority. The government issued gun sits cooly on his hip, a flash of black metal. "Aaron Baldwin was a good man."

Ahh. That's why he's here. He thinks he knows something. Or he's grasping at straws. Hoping there's no way his buddy is as bad as the criminals he hunts down. He's putting on a show, trying to elicit something out of me.

"Got stuck with his cases, huh?" I close out of the news app I had been scrolling through on my phone. Locking the screen, I shove the device in my pocket before standing to be level with the agent in front of me. "Listen, pal," I start. "I didn't know your friend, he came in a few times to chat, try to get me to talk or whatever and then one day I see him on the news." I shake my head. "Sheesh. And you guys act like we're the bad guys." I make a show of shaking my head with a bit of sympathy and just the right amount of judgment.

The new agent grows annoyed, his fingers tightening, his stance becoming more and more rigid by the second.

"If you did something, DelGado," he wags a finger toward me. "You'll go down for it. I'm going to find out what you did."

The grin on my face only grows as his annoyance with me does.

I shrug my shoulders. "I have no idea what you're talking about."

A ruddy color rises on his face as he glares at me.

"But do come back," I add. "If you get a warrant."

"Your ship is not tight, DelGado," He growls. The anger boiling inside of him has grown since he walked through those glass doors. He's threatening to burst with the animosity inside him. "I'm going to take you down."

I brush off his dull threat. The only words that actually cling to my mind are *your ship is not tight.*

What the fuck does that mean?

Does my organization have a leak?

Chapter Seventeen

RHEA

Gian disappears on me again.

He says he's working, sends text messages to my phone to check-in on me periodically, but the communication between us is limited. I feel him slide into bed in the middle of the night, his warm body pressed up against me, but then he's gone before I wake up in the morning.

I'm not sure how much sleep he's getting, how long he rests his eyes curled up next to me. I wonder if he's exhausted from sheer lack of rest. I can't fathom how much he's working, or what he's doing to put a stop to whatever threat hangs over our lives.

I can't figure out if it will always be like this. Is peace even a possibility?

I'm baking chocolate chip cookies and considering making

cannoli when the doorbell rings. Baking is my stress relief. I like to throw my emotions into a mixing bowl, beating out all of my aggressions and turning them into something else. Today, I'm on a sugar kick.

Elena's stands at the threshold when I swing open the front door. She's wearing a long-sleeved jacket wrapped tightly around her body and a pair of large sunglasses hides her eyes. She called me yesterday to see if I was available to write thank you cards with her. My wedding has since passed and I haven't sent the cards out, much to Elena's dismay. With work, studying for the bar, and now adding marriage into the mix, I just didn't have the time or energy to write the thank-you notes.

"Hey," I greet, swinging the door open for her to come in.

Her lips are pressed thin when she looks at me. "Don't freak out," she whispers, sliding the thick-rimmed sunglasses down the bridge of her nose, revealing dark bruises. The shadows circled her right eye, extending over the bridge of her nose. It's large and mean looking and I wince as soon as I see it.

"What happened?" I ask, but deep down I already know the answer.

My father isn't a good man. He's controlling and vindictive. He drinks too much and doesn't like it when he doesn't get his way.

Most of the time he took his anger out on me. It wasn't always physical, sometimes the screaming matches were enough. Belittling me, telling me how silly and worthless I was made him feel like a man. His strength came from how small he made others feel.

"He's been stressed," she mumbles, quick to defend him.

"Elena," I say, reaching out to embrace her. I'm lucky that my mother instilled a sense of self-worth in me long before I moved into Elena's house, because she has no self-love whatsoever.

"It's fine." she tries to wave me off.

I have a feeling she knows it's not fine though. Why would she come here, with these bruises decorating her face if she didn't want me to know? Especially knowing the position Gian holds in *La Famiglia.* "Elena…" I try again, but she waves me off.

"I just needed a break. It will be fine, Rhea. Don't worry about me."

I shut my mouth, but it doesn't stop me from worrying about her. "I'll get coffee," I tell her, giving Andrew a look as I spin on my heel. Knowingly, he follows me.

"Call my husband," I tell him as I fill two coffee mugs. He gives me a curt nod and pulls out his phone, typing on it furiously.

Elena is sitting at the dining room table sipping coffee when Gian arrives. She hasn't spoken a word of what my father did to her or why. Instead, she chats away about the wedding while addressing the thank you cards. I can barely take my eyes off the damage long enough to write a single card. Dark bruises peek out from beneath the sweater she wears. My stomach sinks more with every moment that we sit here. Where are all the places he hit her?

Gian's face shifts immediately as he takes Elena's appearance in, his eyes scanning over the bruises that mar her normally beautiful face. Gian looks bold, every bit as powerful as he is. A sleek, dark suit covers his body, Armani by the looks of it. A crisp white shirt peeks out from beneath his jacket, an extra button is left undone and there's no tie in sight. His shiny black shoes thud on the hardwood as he makes his way toward us.

There's a layer of foundation covering her skin and still the dark circle of the bruising shines through.

"What happened?" My husband growls at my stepmother. Elena flinches at his tone. He's being too harsh for a woman who was just beaten to the pulp. Gian swipes a hand through his slicked back dark hair, loosening the gel that holds the strands in place.

When she doesn't answer, his eyes shift to me instead. "Rhea?"

"I don't know," I tell him. "You're being aggressive, Gi—"

"I don't think I am," he cuts me off. "Elena," he redirects his attention back to my stepmother, lowering his voice and trying to temper himself. "Did Joe do this?"

Elena shrinks under his gaze. Her role as the dutiful wife prevents her from turning on my father. Saying anything bad would go against the image she created, the bubble she so carefully lives in.

My heart breaks for her.

No one deserves to live like this, afraid of their husband, adapting themselves for his needs. That's old world shit, a belief system from when women weren't perceived as equal.

"Elena," I say in the most soothing voice I can manage. "Tell us. You're safe here."

Her eyes dance between Gian and I, still unsure of what she should say or do. "It was an accident," she finally settles on saying.

Gian laughs, a bitter sound leaving his lips. "You don't accidentally punch your wife, Elena," he sneers. "Tell me what he did before I go over there and get it out of him myself."

"Gian!" I hiss. Jesus, does he have no bedside manners?

Elena pales at his words. She wraps her arms around herself, backing further into her chair as if trying to make space between herself and my husband on the other side of the table.

"Last chance, Elena," he says, ignoring my pleas for him to calm down.

When Elena doesn't answer, he spins on his heel, walking back toward the door.

"Wait," she calls out to him. "He's been irritated lately," she finally tells Gian. "Says he's under a lot of pressure... from you."

Gian scoffs, his hands coming to settle on his hips. "That's not an excuse, Elena." He sighs heavily, dragging a hand through his hair. "Okay, I'm going to have a talk with him." He turns, ready to leave again when Elena shouts, breaking into a sob.

"No," she cries. "He'll kill me."

"Elena," I try to cut in, but Gian doesn't let me.

"I'll kill him first."

Gian is out the door again, no goodbye or soft words, just a storm of anger and he's gone. Elena's head droops across the table from me. The sadness seeping from her is overwhelming.

Tears threaten to well up in my eyes as I watch her. Who told this woman she deserved to be treated like this?

"Elena," I whisper, doing my best to hold my emotions back, keeping the tears sealed away. Her own waterlogged eyes look up to me in response. "Why do you let him treat you like this?"

She shrugs her shoulders in a pathetic motion. Swallowing hard, her eyes find mine to answer. "He's my husband."

"So he's allowed to do whatever the fuck he wants?" I'm trying not to yell at her, trying not to let my anger show. But I am angry, the emotion pools inside my belly, threatening to spill over in a loud cursing rage of words. I don't want to scream at my stepmother though, that doesn't make me any better than my father.

I just want her to love herself.

I wish she saw herself the way I see her. She's beautiful, inside and out. She's a wonderful mother, a caring soul. Christopher and I never went without, never felt unheard or unseen. She made sure to come to every play, soccer game, and ceremony. She is a good person, and she lets herself be treated like shit.

"What would you say if Gian did that to me?" I ask. "If I came to your home sporting bruises like the ones you wear."

A delicate finger comes to her face, tracing over the discoloration caused by my father's hands. "I was raised in a different time," she says weakly. "I was told my husband is always right." Her eyes shift to meet mine. "I don't have your spark, your perseverance. I don't know where you got it, Rhea, but it wasn't from me." A long stream of air blows from her lips.

I reach across the table, taking her hand into my own. "Elena, I don't know who made you feel like this is the kind of love you deserve, but it's not."

Her glassy eyes find mine and we pause for a moment. Sitting in silence, holding hands, and both letting the words sink in.

"I'm sorry." She finally says.

"For what?"

"I should have stopped this." She waves a hand, motioning around my home. "I should have stood up for you, instead I stood by while your father used you." She hiccups on a soft sob, her guilt spilling over with her admission.

I don't blame Elena at all. She's just another pawn in my father's games and regardless, if she would have said something to him, nothing would have changed.

The men in our lives always get their way in the end.

Chapter Eighteen

GIAN

The pizza shop only has a few customers scattered about, the lack of a crowd is one of the reasons I like to work out of this location.

Sal slides a small cup of espresso over to me as I wait. He gives me a solemn look and a pat on the shoulder. Sal's known me since I was a kid, and my father for even longer. When his son was arrested for dealing coke, my father handled the case, pleading it down to only a few community service hours. When his restaurant was on the brink of going under, I gave him the funds to get it going again. In return, I have my small office here and he gives me too much food.

The espresso machine was a bonus. Sal and I both have a taste for a good brew.

"Whatever it is, kid," he tells me, he's probably the only person I allow to call me kid. "It will work out. You always figure it out, hmm?"

Figure it out. That sentence is like a motto to me. Words Massimo yelled at me practically every time I opened my mouth.

I had asked Massimo for help with a problem I was having on my route once. Long before I had my sights set on his seat at the table, and before I knew the kind of monster he was. Back then I still idolized the man, still hung on his every word. I was dealing, upgrading from pot to white powder. I had my route carved out, handed over to me from two low-level soldiers. The two guys who had to give up customers so the consigliere's son could have a job weren't thrilled about me being there. They made it hard for me every step of the way, sneaking onto my block to sell or undercut me.

Massimo told me to 'figure it out.' He slung the words at me like my problems weren't worth his time. It was a lesson I needed to learn though, because my problems weren't worth bothering the boss. I was low-level, the only reason I even had access to the man was because of my father's position and long term friendship with him.

So I figured it out.

I waited for them to step over the line and then I beat the shit out of them. I got each of them alone, giving me the advantage and avoiding a 2-on-1 scenario. I was a scrappy kid, lean and muscular from regular sparring sessions with Theo. They got a few hits in, but it was me who knocked them out.

They didn't bother me again after that.

Nothing was handed to me. Everything I have was earned, my kingdom was built with blood, sweat, and tears. My time on the street was just the building blocks of my empire.

The older generation, Joe's generation, see me as a spoiled kid. They built the city with nothing but the clothes on their back and the wild dreams running through their heads. They think because I was born to a man of power, of privilege, that I don't know what it means to work hard. Or what it means to lose the things and people I love to *La Famiglia.* As if I didn't bury my mother not too long ago.

"FBI agent fired after evidence was found linking him to a murder investigation." The TV mounted in the corner of the shop blares. One of Sal's waitresses has her hands on her hips as she watches the story unfold. Her lips twitch in shock as she listens. "How horrible," I hear her whisper. "Our own FBI."

I chuckle softly to myself. If only she knew.

Joe comes through the front doors. He ambles over to my table, his soft belly jiggling as he enters. "You wanted to see me?" he asks, his voice gruff and his hands coming to rest on his hips in an assertive gesture.

"Sit," I wave my hand to the chair across from me, telling him to take a seat. "Coffee?" I ask, an attempt at making him comfortable before I toss my accusation at him.

He nods his head and Sal grabs the pot from his waitress,

filling a ceramic mug with the dark liquid for Joe.

"So, you like to hit women?" I ask casually, taking a sip of my espresso.

Joe's face pales at my accusation. "I-what did-" spittle flies from his lips as he stutters over his words. Red has colored his cheeks, his embarrassment making itself apparent. Clearly he didn't expect to get called out when he arrived here. The disrespectful bastard should have gotten here sooner, should have called me boss when spoke to me. He should have done a lot of things differently.

There's a steak knife on the table. Sal had placed the settings for me in case we decided to eat. The man never knows what my meetings will consist of or what I'll need, so he normally sets the table, brings coffee and pastries his wife bakes. He's always trying to feed me. I fiddle with the black wooden handle of the knife as Joe talks, he's going to spout out an excuse. A reason why she deserves to be hit, or that she fell. Something stupid, I'm sure of it.

With a quick move, I lift the knife and bring it down onto the hand that rests on the red and white checkered tablecloth.

I watch as his eyes go wide and a scream escapes his lips.

The few patrons in the restaurant whip their heads over toward us, staring in shock at the man pinned to the table with a knife in his hand. Without being told, Rafi goes to calm them, sliding cash across the table in exchange for not calling 911, then shooing them out of the shop.

Sal doesn't even twitch as it goes down, instead he wipes his hand on a rag and locks up the doors after the last customer leaves.

"Now, Joe," I tell him, my eyes watching the way his face contorts in pain. He holds his wrist with the opposite hand, probably wondering if he should pull the knife out or not. "I don't want to hear any lies, understood?"

Joe frantically nods his head in response, his eyes glued to the knife. "I hit her," he says, the truth spilling from his lips. "She was being a bitch, so I smacked her around. That what you want to hear?" he says in a frenzied rush.

I grasp the knife again, yanking it from his hand, causing him to scream loudly.

"Don't fucking touch your wife," I tell him.

He sobs across from me, grasping his bleeding hand against his chest. Fucking little bitch.

"We don't beat women. If I find out you touched her again, I'll kill you. Do you understand?" I ask, the last word leaving my lips in a low growl.

His glassy eyes find me. Rhea must take after her mother because she looks nothing like this fucker. The thought that she came from him, that something so beautiful could come from something so foul blows my mind.

"Understood," he says.

The house is loud when I come home. Banging comes from the kitchen, metal clashing against the marble countertops. I don't see Elena when I enter the room, just Rhea. Loose sweatpants hang from her hips and her hair is tied up in a messy bun with a very '90s looking scrunchie. She wears a pale blue tank top that hugs her curves.

I've never seen her not put together. She always goes to work in a full face of makeup and designer clothes. This is the first time she's looked casual with me.

Her emerald eyes flicker to me as I enter. "How'd it go?" she asks immediately, straightening her spine. Her fire is back, I can almost see it radiating from her. She was scared after the drive-by. It loosened her, let her fall into my grasp more easily. But now it's back, burning as her gaze lands on me, waiting for my answer. I can already tell we're going to fight tonight.

"Fine," I tell her, leaning against the counter while I watch her work on rolling dough. I'm assuming the crash I heard came from the two metal baking pans laying on the floor behind her. She ignores them, as if trying to hide whatever emotion made her throw them in the first place. "Everything okay here?" I ask, a small smirk rising on my lips.

Her face snaps back up, her eyes meeting mine. "I was angry," she says, nodding to the pans.

"I get that," I tell her, trying to be slightly more sensitive. Not that I'm avoiding an argument, hate fucking is definitely on the menu tonight. "Did Elena leave?"

"Yeah," her eyes dip, sadness brimming at the edges.

I step closer, moving so I'm behind her, wrapping my arms

around her waist. "He's an ass," I tell her. "And it's taken care of."

Her body stills in my grasp, her head turning slightly to peek at me through a veil of dark hair. "You didn't…"

"No. I didn't kill him. I'm not a monster and he's a made man."

Rhea releases a long breath. "I don't want him to die…" she mumbles, her gaze avoiding mine. "But I want him to be punished." She sounds sad and disappointed when she whispers the words to me.

"You think it's wrong that you want to see him punished?" I ask, pressing a light kiss to her temple.

"Yes," she breathes. "He's… my father."

I never had that feeling with my family, my parents and siblings have always been good to me. I've never had a moment where I wished anything bad on them. But Massimo was different. He was like a second father to me, his son like a brother. I trusted him indefinitely. But his affection was conditional, based on how much I provided him. When I didn't provide any value, when I fucked up, he withheld his approval, the things I craved. And when that wasn't enough, he would pit Theo and I against each other, manipulating us until we'd beat each other up. That way he never had to lay a finger on us.

"It's okay to want to see him punished." I tell her, "And trust me, *cara,* he's regretting his actions."

Her glossy eyes find mine, assessing me. Probably wondering if she should be sick or turned on by my words. "Thank you," she whispers.

"Rhea…"I trail off. "Did he ever…"

"Don't ask." She cuts me off. "Don't ask things you don't want to know the answer to."

Her cryptic answer tells me what I want to know. He hurt her. I want to know the gory details, I want it mapped out hit for hit, so I can do everything to him that he did to her. I want to make him pay for everything he's ever done to Rhea.

"Gian?" she asks softly.

"Yeah?"

"Do you remember when you were telling me you could handle that case for me? You said you would handle it outside of… the law." She pauses, swallowing hard. "Can you do that?"

My little law-abiding citizen is switching over to the dark side. I don't know if I'm proud or concerned. The look in her eyes is sad, but stern. She's realizing that justice doesn't work her way. That's why men like my father have jobs, men who talk the talk and have connections. Right and wrong mean nothing in this world.

If you want justice, you have to take it into your own hands.

"You sure you want that?" I ask. "Once you go that route, there's no coming back."

She nods her head slowly. "Yes," she whispers. "This girl deserves justice."

Chapter Nineteen

RHEA

My eyes are glued to the news. The website of every local station is on my screen. I can't turn my gaze away. I'm waiting for something to break, for someone to realize that the men who beat and raped a nineteen-year-old student were punished. I'm waiting to see the announcement that karma happened and they got what was coming to them.

But I'm karma and I sealed their fate.

Guilt and anxiety pool in my stomach, making me hate myself for what I asked Gian to do. Does anyone deserve to have the Providence Mafia unleashed on them? If anyone, it would be these guys.

But still, does that make it right?

I believe in the law, believe in the government, believe it should protect people.

But it doesn't.

No one was there when I was the one being beaten. When my father's fists were pounding into my stomach and my skull. Leaving marks and bruises along my skin. No one was there when I was in college, throwing back shots of vodka and being manhandled into a bedroom up the stairs.

No one noticed.

No one cared.

There was something about Gian seeking justice for Elena, how he protected her. Maybe there is good in the world, it just comes from the most unlikely places.

I'm getting impatient seeing nothing being reported. Gian said he would take care of it last night and then he left the kitchen to make a call. I assumed that was the call to plan the hit, or the beating, whatever they call it.

But nothing's happening. Nothing is on the news at all.

The door to the law office swings open and I hear Gemma's voice greet whoever enters. My eyes are still glued to the screen as the thud of boots comes closer to my office. It's not until Christopher's large body blocks my entryway that I finally divert my attention from the screen.

"Hey," I say, but my voice comes out strange, higher pitched than normal.

"Hey," he repeats, coming further into my office to plop down into the seat across from my desk. "Just came to see how married life was treating you, you haven't been around the house in a while." He gives me an accusing look, which is unusual for my brother.

Christopher has been my best friend since I was ten years old. My hatred for our father isn't lost on him. He knows the abuse I suffered in that house, how my sperm donor made me feel unwanted and like a waste of space. I wonder if he would have loved me more if I had a dick, or if being the mistress's baby was enough to make me worthless that my gender mattered little.

"It's good," I say, trying to calm my nerves.

"You're shaking," he says, pointing to my leg that bounces up and down at a quick pace.

Fuck. I try to calm myself, slapping a hand to my shaking leg to stop it.

I don't want to tell Christopher what I asked my new husband to do. I'm scared to admit that I went beyond the law for this one. My skin feels dirty just thinking about it.

I studied the law, I believe in its purpose, its power. And yet, I betrayed it by asking Gian to seek revenge on those boys.

"I'm fine," I tell him. "I swear."

My hand moves to the cross dangling from my neck, my fingers tracing over the worn pendant, seeking some kind of comfort to guide me through this moment.

I wonder if my mother would be proud of the woman I've become. What would she say if she knew what I'd done?

"Is he treating you okay?" Chris asks, his eyes studying me as if he's looking for damage, making sure I'm still in pristine condition.

"Yes, Chris," I huff. It's not like my brother would do anything if he wasn't treating me well. He watched our father use me as a punching bag for years and never did a thing about it. I love my brother, he's my best friend, but he's a follower. Whether it's my father or my husband, he's not going to stand up for me.

He nods his head, "Okay, well I just wanted to stop by." He looks defeated by this conversation and to be fair, I'm not giving him much.

I'm too distracted. My mind can't focus on him, instead it's thinking about the fact that I might be a murderer.

"I'm sorry," I mutter. "I'm just distracted."

"Well, I'll let you get back to it." He stands slowly, heading for my door. "Love you, Rhe," he says over his shoulder, giving me one last look before he leaves.

I'm still shaking, still focused on what I asked Gian to do. I want to call him, I need some confirmation that it happened… or to stop it.

"I have to go." I tell Gemma abruptly, grabbing my cell phone and running for the door.

"Okay…" she mumbles as I run out of my office.

Andrew leaps from his chair when he sees me, following me out of the building, matching my brisk pace. "Where are we going?" he asks, his cool demeanor cracks ever so slightly at my frantic movement.

"Just the SUV." I open the door to the Escalade, getting into the back seat and heaving a breath. "Can I have a minute?" I ask Andrew before he has a chance to sit. He nods his agreement, a skeptic look crossing his face for only a second.

I pull out my iPhone, bringing up Gian's name and hitting call. My heart is thrumming in my chest at a quick pace, threatening to break through my rib cage with its pounding. My breathing is shaky and my head is spinning with thoughts.

What if I'm too late? What if it's already done?

What if Gian's men went too far, mixed up the message, what if they killed those kids?

Does their crime deserve death? Have I suddenly become the judge, jury, and executioner?

I'm panting by the time Gian answers the phone, a sweet greeting leaving his lips. "I'm surprised," he says. "You never call me."

It's true. I never call my husband. Our affection toward each other doesn't extend much past the bedroom. We only have one form of communication, skin to skin, body to body.

"Did you…" I can't say what I asked him to do, not on the phone. He has codes, I think, I've heard him talk in cryptic messages over the phone. Giving Gio weird instructions. Picking up the cannoli, grabbing the coffee, using names and codes for things that I can't place.

"Get those tomatoes for you?" he asks. It takes me a minute to realize we're not talking about tomatoes, that this is code for did he do the job I asked for.

"Yeah," I whisper. "Did you?"

I hear him inhale a breath before answering me, my head spirals waiting for him, needing to know the answer. Needing to know what I did.

"No," he says.

All the air in my lungs rushes from me. My eyes well, brimming with tears. "Don't do it." I say.

"I know, *cara*." His voice purrs through the phone.

"Ho—"

"You don't have the heart. And I don't mean that as an insult. You're a good person, Rhea, you believe in justice. Don't change that."

"I thought…" I heave a breath, not sure if I'm thankful for him not listening to me or angry. This case is going to suck. Getting her a lawyer alone will be hard, not to mention that once she has a lawyer, the case will drag on, and who knows if she'll ever get justice. But should I circumvent the process?

"Thank you," I whisper.

"Do you need anything else?" he asks.

"Will you be home for dinner?"

"Do you want me home for dinner?" he answers my question with his own.

"Yes."

For the first time since we've been married, I'm excited to cook for Gian. My appreciation for him has grown in the last forty-eight hours. First with his protectiveness over Elena and now with today's *situation*.

I still feel sick in the stomach when I think about what I asked him to do.

I don't think I could have lived with myself had he actually gone through with it. Had something happened to those kids, no matter how vile and horrible they are, I would have hated myself for it.

"It smells amazing," Gian practically moans as he walks through the front door. The corners of his lips lift into a small smile. He looks more pleasant than normal as he waltzes into the kitchen.

I'm used to the hard lines of his features, a frown marring his face. But today he looks peaceful, happy even.

"Meatballs," I tell him, stirring the sauce filled with the homemade meatballs I made. "My mother's recipe."

The soles of his leather loafers thud against the hardwood as he makes his way over to me. An arm wraps around my waist as he comes behind me, pressing a long kiss to my temple. "Amazing," he says.

He holds this position, keeping me wrapped in his arms as I stir the sauce. Only letting me go when it comes time to plate the food. He helps me then, grabbing two bowls from the cabinet and holding them while I spoon the spaghetti noodles, sauce, and meatballs in.

"Can I take you somewhere?" he asks softly as I'm spinning

noodles around on my fork. "After we're done." He adds.

"Sure."

After we eat, he leads me to his BMW. We're both silent as he drives through the streets of Providence, we're in a weird place between love and hate. Something has shifted between us, I no longer want to slap him across the face. The sight of him doesn't make my blood boil. The sound of his voice doesn't turn the edges of my vision red.

He pulls us into Carousel Park, a small area a few miles from the city zoo. It's late, the clock on the dashboard tells me it's after ten already. The large carousel that this area boasts is already closed and the empty parking lot we pull into confirms it.

"What are we doing here?" I ask as Gian parks the car in front of the spinning attraction.

He smiles, the grin reaching all the way to the corners of his eyes. His gaze flickers between me and the carousel. "Come on," he says, swinging open his door and leaving the car.

I'm not sure what we're doing in an empty park after ten p.m., but I don't question Gian as I exit the BMW. Cool Providence air greets me and I pull my cardigan tighter, following him toward the merry-go-round.

Gian stops in front of it, looking up at the monster of a ride. An emotion that I can't place flickers across his dark eyes; joy, I think. "Why are we here?" I ask again.

Suddenly the carousel comes to life, the lights flickering on and music begins to flow from the speakers. The sound startles me and I jump, gripping on to Gian for support.

A soft laugh escapes his lips as he wraps an arm around my back, steadying me.

"All set, boss." I hear, my eyes scanning across the empty area to a slim man talking to Gian. I was too distracted wondering why we were here to even notice him.

Gian extends a hand to the contraption, waiting for me to step on first.

"What are we *doing here?*" I ask again, still waiting for an explanation, some kind of reasoning to why we're here.

Gian still doesn't answer me, instead he leads me up onto the carousel and tells me to pick a horse, any horse. I choose a cream one with a dark chocolate covered mane and a teal saddle. Swinging a leg over, I get up on the horse right before the thing starts to move. I whip my head around, looking for the guy who was just here.

"Self-timer," Gian says. "I had him set it and give us some privacy."

"Oh." It drifts slowly, chugging along at a lazy pace. The horses move vertically at the same slow pace, gliding up and down the poles that hold them. Gian doesn't jump on a horse, instead he stands next to mine, his hand resting on the small of my back and following as my horse gallops along.

"My mom used to take me here." Gian says, and finally I feel like my question has been answered. "She loved it." He smiles. "Even after Gio and Gemma were born she used to bring me here just the two of us."

His dark eyes are shining, a happy emotion swirling around in them. Gian doesn't share much with me. He doesn't talk about his job, his family, mostly everything I know about him comes from Gemma.

"That sounds really nice." I whisper, "Thank you for sharing this with me."

We're silent for a moment, just settled next to each other, swaying with the movement of the ride. "I bought this place after she died." He says with a laugh. "I didn't tell my siblings, they'd think it's stupid."

"I doubt that." I tell him. Each of the DelGado siblings mourns their mother differently, and I get that. Grief isn't the same for everyone. I was silent after my mother died, not wanting to talk to anyone. My heart was torn to shreds from watching her waste away.

"This is my cross," he says. My face contorts, not understanding what he means. A finger lifts, touching the gold cross hanging from my neck softly. As a reflex, I bring my own hand to it, my finger dusting across the gold.

"Oh," I whisper.

"You carry your mother around your neck, and I… well, I guess I just buy her favorite place." A quiet laugh leaves his lips.

"I think she'd love it," I tell him.

"Yeah, maybe."

"How often do you come here?" I ask.

"Every week," he answers. A blush rises to Gian's cheeks and I think it's the first time I've seen him embarrassed. He doesn't show emotion, doesn't get sentimental around me, except for here on this carousel.

I think this might be my favorite place too.

Chapter Twenty

GIAN

Rhea's emerald eyes shine under the light of the carousel, flecks of green and gold gazing up at me from where she's seated on the fake horse. Swirls of dark hair fall over her shoulder, and her lips twist up into the sweetest smile while the horse rises and falls.

Before I can control my hand, it's weaved through her hair, wrapping the dark strands around and pulling her neck taut. Her throat bobs and those sweet green eyes meet mine. I lean in slowly, devouring the sight of her right now, like this, at my mercy before I go in for the kiss. I suck in her bottom lip, bringing it between my teeth and nipping at her gently.

I can feel her breath hitch at the action. My strong, beautiful woman likes pain. Her heart rate spikes, I can feel it when I bring my free hand to her throat, I feel every subtle change in her. Every breath that comes through her pretty lips.

I have the itch to squeeze my fingers around the delicate column of her throat, and I think if I did, she'd enjoy it. My little monster is a glutton for pain, for punishment. I think that's why she keeps letting me between her legs. That, or being with me has changed her, made her fall in love with the monster under her bed when she should be running.

"You make me feel…" she whispers, her voice husky.

"What, *bella*, tell me what I make you feel?"

Her thin fingers grip tightly around the saddle on the horse as she watches me, her mouth just slightly open. "Everything." She finishes. "You make me feel everything."

I lean forward and claim her lips. She matches my frenzied pace, our mouths meld together, tongues clash. With both arms, I grip around her waist, lifting and pulling her off the pretend horse. Legs wrap around me as I carry her over to the bench. The carousel still spins, the lights twinkling above us. I'm thankful for the fitted pencil skirt she wears as I shift it up her hips enough for me to grab a hold of the scrap of lace that covers her slit, tugging the fabric down and pocketing it.

Her eyes are hazy, full of lust as she watches me.

"Gian," she moans, "We're in public."

"I don't give a fuck."

She's already wet for me, her pussy throbbing with need as I slip a finger through her hot slit. A sweet moan leaves her mouth and those pretty eyes watch me work. Dragging her wetness up her slit, I swirl my pointer finger over her swollen bundle of nerves, eliciting the prettiest noises from her lips.

"Gian," she pleads. "We're…"

"I know where we are, *bella,* and I already told you I don't care. Now, stop teasing me and let me have this sweet pussy of yours." I thrust a finger into her entrance as the words leave my lips. Her mouth opens, rounding into a soft O.

I bring my mouth to her wet heat, licking my way through her folds as she cries softly above me. My tongue finds its way to her clit, lapping circles around the bud. Rhea squirms, her lips fully open and her eyes tightly closed.

"Look at me," I command her, moving my mouth away from her clit long enough to growl the request before returning to my torturous sucking.

She's crying out louder now, moans and incomprehensible words. I can feel her tightening around my fingers, her pussy gripping onto me. She's so fucking close.

"That's it, baby." I coo. "Be a good girl and cum for me now."

She explodes on my fingers, her juices dripping down my hand as I continue thrusting my digits in and out of her. I give her clit one last nip as she cries out. Her breathing is ragged, uneven, but I'm not quite done.

My cock is hard in my slacks, threatening to burst free. She's still panting when I flip her over so she's on her knees on the bench. "Grab on," I instruct her and her hands come to rest on the back of the bench.

I free my cock from the black slacks and line it up with her entrance. "Are you ready for me?"

Green eyes peer at me over her shoulder through a veil of black curls. "Yes," she breathes.

I push into her, giving her a second to adjust to me. I can feel her walls pulse around me, squeezing my cock.

"Fuck," she moans.

"That's it, baby." I thrust into her, continuing my assault of her pussy as the carousel spins us around. I snake my hand forward, a trail of goosebumps rising along her spine. I fist a handful of dark curls, tugging so her neck stretches back. I can see her face over the top of her head, her eyes squeeze tight and she pushes back against me.

"I want you to come all over my cock, baby girl, I want to hear you moan and cry while I fuck you."

She whimpers, a soft plea leaving her lips before I feel the walls of her pussy clench, squeezing me tightly. "I'm coming," she cries. I drop her hair, reaching forward instead to slap my hand over her mouth, softening her cries as she explodes over my cock.

I follow her over the cliff as her pussy milks me, draining every last drop of my orgasm.

We're panting as I collapse in the seat next to her, tucking myself away and helping her slide her skirt back down.

Her hazy, love-drunk eyes find me and a soft smile rises on

her lips. "Fuck," she mutters. "Why was that so hot?"

Pain beats through my chest as she leans in for another kiss. Here I am holding her, laying claim to her when I'm just as bad as her father, the man I claim to protect her from.

"Rhea," I breathe, "I'm sorry."

"For what?" she asks. Her eyes are hazy as she peers up at me.

"For this." I wrap her hand in mine, moving my fingers over the rings that rest on her left ring finger. "For chaining you to me, when you never asked for this."

Her body stills at my confession, her breath dying in her throat, her head dropping. It's a long moment before she speaks again. "I shouldn't forgive you," she says, a boldness behind her words. "I should hate you for everything you've done." I can feel the anger in her voice as she speaks. "But I don't hate you. I think someone broke you." She admits, her eyes finding mine again. "I think someone made you believe you had to be like this, strong and fucking menacing. No one ever let you be yourself. Do you even know who you are, Gian? Who are you when you're not changing yourself to be this... this mastermind? This man who manipulates and controls everything around him?" She looks at me expectantly, wanting an answer to her questions.

But I don't have one. I've always been this. I've always taken control, always manipulated others to do my bidding, to fit my goals.

I was raised to be like this, and not by my parents. Not by the immigrants who wanted a better life for their children and just fell into *La Famiglia*. My boss raised me this way, through well-timed comments and the crack of his fists. Through his basement fighting ring, to the hits I took when he forced me down there, showed me a man, and told me only one of us will leave there tonight.

He turned me into a monster at a young age. Groomed and manipulated me to be a boss. Told me everyone was the enemy. The only people I had were myself, and the men I surrounded myself with. The men who sliced their palms and took an oath. The men as committed to this brotherhood as me.

I was trained to be cold-blooded and calculated.

"I'm the boss."

She's not amused by my response. She doesn't understand what I worked for, what I sacrificed for this position. How many friends' funerals I had to attend, tossing flowers on shiny black coffins. I buried my own mother because of this family.

This fucking oath.

"You don't have to be." She cries out, slapping a manicured hand down on her thigh. "You could walk away from it all and just be done." She looks like she believes the words when she says them.

"How sheltered are you? You think you can just walk away from all of this?" I wave my hands around us, to the world we live in. Suddenly the carousel feels less sweet and nostalgic. Instead, the darkness takes over, seeping its inky gloom into us.

Fire ignites in those emerald eyes when they find me again.

"That's not fair. I was raised in this just as much as you."

"No, *bella*," I laugh. "You were raised to be protected," I tell her, moving close enough to brush my nose against her soft cheek. "You were clothed, and fed, and fucking sheltered until a man like me came along to take you off your father's hands. Sure, you had it rough, daddy hit mommy, but at the end of the day you were protected."

Rage fills her eyes, her neck has craned itself back so she can get a good look at me while she glares. Her fingers grip around the handles on the plastic horse. "I wasn't protected, Gian. My father didn't want me. I learned to love by licking crumbs off the floor. Lunging for any morsel of affection. Any drop of desire I could get." She holds eye contact with me while she talks, letting each of her words rip into my chest. "You asked why I was so mad about that case, why I wanted so badly to seek revenge for that girl? Because I've been her. Because I know what it's like to want to be loved so bad you'll do anything. You'll follow boys into a dirty house. Drink the alcohol they pour down your throat. You're so fucking desperate for any ounce of affection that you let them get you so wasted you couldn't say no if you wanted to. And when the next morning comes around and shame pools in your stomach, there's nothing you can do about it."

"Rhea," I breathe, red clouding the edges of my vision. "If someone hurt you…"

"No." She stops me. "Everyone's hurt me. You included. I've been beaten, discarded, traded away. Every man in my life has let me down."

"No." I'm the one to interrupt this time. "I'm not letting you down, *cara*. So we married in a shitty situation. That doesn't have to mean anything. You want to play the victim card, do it, live in the cloud of self-pity, but don't cry to me, because you could be a fucking queen. You could rule the fucking kingdom with me, but you're too busy feeling sorry for yourself."

She stills, her mouth turning into a thin line on her pretty face.

"Did that finally shut you up?" I ask.

"You're an ass." She deadpans.

"So you've said."

I bring my mouth to the crook of her neck, sucking on the sensitive flesh. "Tell me what you want, Rhea, tell me anything you fucking want."

"A divorce."

Chapter Twenty-one

RHEA

The bed is cold and empty when I wake up. Not that I think Gian ever came to join me. His opposition to my divorce comment was quite strong. Apparently, I was supposed to forgive him, erase the guilt that sits in his head but not ask for any resolution. No change, no happiness for me.

His apology seemed heartfelt, but it held no weight to it, no willingness to do better.

He wasn't going to change.

Love wouldn't turn him into a better person, he wasn't willing to try to make this an actual marriage. He just wants to have his way and crawl into bed with me at the same time.

But he can't have both with me.

I have no desire to go into the office today, especially knowing I'll have to see his family. Not that he talks to Gemma much anyway, and if Giuseppe knew about our marriage problems, I doubt he'd say anything.

The silent treatment from my husband shouldn't make me feel anything. This marriage is a fraud, built off nothing substantial. Whether or not we're together, there's nothing here for us. So there's no reason for me to be having feelings. Even with the logical part of my brain telling me this, my chest still aches.

The tension between us had eased in the past month, our connection had grown closer even if it was mostly between the sheets, but now, it's snapped like a twig.

I take a scalding shower to wash the shame of the public sex from my body. Gian brings out a different version of me. His fingers ignite a fire along my skin, turning me into someone that craves his touch. I've become a Gian DelGado addict. I need a rehab center, stat. The water runs down the drain, washing all my sins along with it.

It's forty-five minutes before I'm out the door. If I was a good employee, I would already be at the office doing trial prep for Giuseppe's latest case. But I'm exhausted, my bones ache and my body feels sluggish.

I shoot Christopher to meet me at Starbucks and tell Andrew to drive me there before we head to the office. My concern about being on time for work has faded, what's my father-in-law going to do? Fire me?

Unlikely, and even if he did, it doesn't matter.

Even after the sweet nectar of the gods begins to trickle

through my system, I feel irritability soaking in. Anger at myself, for the life I have. For years, since I was a child, I've just been focusing on getting to the next step, fighting through each stage with the promise that one day it would get better. One day it would be easier.

But that day never came.

And now here I am, twenty-five years old and married to the boss of the Providence Mafia.

I don't even recognize myself.

I wanted to be better than this, to do more with my life. My mother had told me I could be whatever I wanted when I grew up, and I believed her. Instead, here I am at the mercy of a man. A man that I didn't even choose for myself.

Could I love Gian? Maybe.

But that doesn't erase how we got here. What he did to get me under his thumb. I feel betrayed, every person in my life who should have been there for me, taken care of me, every single one has disappointed me.

My parents, Christopher, and now Gian. I feel like an inanimate object, passed around to the pleasure of my owners.

I wasn't lying last night when I uttered the word *divorce*, even if I know it will never happen. But I need freedom, I need the ability to choose. My free will has been stripped away from me between my father and Gian and no matter how many orgasms my husband gives me, it won't erase that fact.

I want to be selfish. I want to enjoy my life. Feel the sun on my skin, the sand between my toes. I want to experience everything with no mafia intervention.

The coffee scalds my tongue as I sip it. My brother enters the coffee shop in a pair of faded jeans and a white t-shirt. He's dressed down, likely heading to a construction site after this. He gives me a small smile when he finds me seated by the front window.

"Got you a cup," I tell him, pushing a paper cup of hot coffee toward him.

He smiles gratefully as he sits down across from me. "I'm glad you called."

I can't blame Christopher for the downfall of my life, for the feelings racing through my head. He's never done anything to hurt me. "I'm sorry," I tell him, "Everything's just been…"

"Hectic?" He finishes for me, bringing the cup of coffee to his lips.

"Hectic." I repeat. "I'm sorry for being so short with you the other day. You seemed like you wanted to talk about something. What was it?"

Christopher shifts uncomfortably, running a hand through his dark hair and avoiding eye contact.

"What's up?" I ask again, sensing something off with my brother.

Chris has always been happy-go-lucky. I've never seen him yell, granted I've never seen him working. I've always known him as the sweet big brother who spends his time trying to make me laugh.

"I messed up, Rhe," he whispers, his eyes still pointed down at the table.

"Okay, what do you mean? I'm sure we can fix it."

"We can't." His voice cracks when he speaks. He twists his fingers together and breathes heavily. "I was pissed, this asshole just walked into our lives and took you, like you were his fucking property. It was ridiculous, and Dad, well Dad wouldn't do a damn thing to protect you. I had to do something to protect you. You're my little sister, Rhe. Ma always told me to look out for you."

"Chris... what did you do?"

"I just wanted to scare him." Finally, his eyes raise to meet mine, their dark as he continues. "His mom was killed like that, a drive-by shooting, I thought... I thought if I made him think that someone could get to you, he'd let you go. He wasn't always this strong, ya know? He's weak, he's human, and I thought if I could scare him enough, he'd just let you go." Christopher looks frantic while he tells me this. His eyes drift around like he's waiting for someone to grab him, to stop him from telling me this.

"What are you saying, Chris?"

"I shot at your house." He shoves his face into the palms of his hands. "I'm sorry, Rhe, I was never going to hurt you."

My body tenses at his words while my mind spirals to process what he's saying. "Why... why would you shoot at me?"

"Not at you!" He tries to clarify quickly. "At no one, it was just to scare him."

"He wasn't there Chris, I was. And Andrew, you could have shot him. Why… I don't understand why you would do that?" I feel the heat rising in my body, coating my vision with a hazy red shade. Why would my brother, my own fucking brother, who I loved and trusted, shoot at my house?

Someone could have been hurt. My blood simmers in my veins, anger coursing through them. I rise quickly, grabbing my purse and sliding it onto my shoulder.

"Please, Rhea," Chris grabs my wrist, his eyes find mine with a pleading look. "Don't tell him."

"Fuck you." I yank my wrist from his grasp. He's another name on the list of people who have failed me.

I'm pissed as I get into the car, fuming as Andrew drives me to the office in silence. I can tell by the nearly empty parking lot that Giuseppe isn't here yet. Only three cars sit in the lot, Gemma's red Lexus, Edie's silver Saturn, and a silver sedan that I'm not sure who it belongs to. I feel less guilty about not being on time.

I want to wish I never met my brother at Starbucks. Wish I would have never heard the words leave his mouth. But I can't unhear them now.

My own brother could have killed me.

My heels have barely hit the pavement when the driver's door of the silver sedan pops open, the trunk lifting at the same time.

The next moment happens quickly. The man exits the car charging toward me. He's wearing all black, his face partially covered with the rim of his black beanie.

My coffee hits the pavement with a thud, splashing up and speckling my legs with the hot liquid. Before I can react to the burning sensation, his arms are on me and something hits the back of my head.

The pain radiates through my skull and I'm falling into blackness.

Faintly I can hear Andrew yelling before it all just turns to nothing but swirling inky darkness.

There's a throbbing in my head. It beats in time with the pounding in my chest. I try to blink my eyes, but they feel heavy and crusted shut. As a reflex, my hands itch to rub them, but there's something in the way, something holding them together, pressed to my back.

It takes a moment, but I finally get my eyes open, blinking through the fluorescent lighting.

I'm sitting up in what looks to be a metal folding chair. The floor is cement, covered in a clear plastic. The sight of the tarp makes my stomach turn. Why would that be here... unless whoever kidnapped me plans to make a mess of me. The ability to clean up easily is needed for torture. I don't know if this knowledge rests in my head from watching too much tv or from the company I keep.

My stomach cartwheels and I swallow hard, willing myself not to vomit.

Each of my ankles is secured to the metal chair. I shake them, wiggle them, but the rope is tied tightly, the fibers cutting into my ankles and giving me no hope of freeing myself. With the way my captor has my legs spread, I'm wishing I wasn't wearing a skirt. I can feel the cool air coming from the vents and sending goose bumps over my bare legs.

I'm vulnerable in this position, tied up and waiting. My heart pounds in my chest, unease whirls in my stomach, the sensation is making me feel achy and like I might throw up. My throat is dry, my tongue weighs a hundred pounds. I need a drink.

How could I have been so stupid to end up here? How did I put myself in such a vulnerable position?

I should have run. A laugh escapes my lips at the thought. The action splits the dry skin and sends an ache through my body, but I can't help it. Could I have run? My father would have found me. He would have brought me back kicking and screaming and then beat the shit out of me for trying to escape.

I wouldn't have made it.

And Gian has no intentions of letting me go, he's made that very clear.

So my life is just a bargaining chip. I'm meant to be tossed around, traded between powerful men, kidnapped and tortured. All because these men think they own me.

And I was dumb enough to think that wasn't true. That I have any amount of free will or control over my life.

I'm just a pawn. And at the end of the day, I'm not the one controlling the board.

The creaking sound that comes from the opening door sends a chill down my spine. My brain is still hazy as the man comes into focus. He has a balding head and a menacing grin. His eyes rake over my body as he stuffs his hands into the pocket of his dark wash jeans.

He looks dirty. Smears of something dark mar his jeans. His shirt has dabs of different colored stains. Red globs of something darken the gray cotton fabric. It could be food. I will myself to believe that it is food. He was eating a hot dog or something, and ketchup dripped. But there's a sinking feeling in my stomach that it's not food.

"Rhea Estella Cabrera." My name rolls off his tongue in an ugly hiss. "You're impossible to get alone, ya know that?" he tells me as he drags another metal chair across the concrete floor. The screeching sound echoes through the room.

I don't want to admit I'm scared. These are the moments that make or break you as a person. My life is flashing before my eyes and I'm not happy with what I'm seeing. What I did in this life wasn't enough. I want more. I want to help people, to win cases. I want to see little dark-haired children running through a grassy backyard.

I want to live, and I haven't gotten that chance yet.

But the fear courses through my veins even with the constant voice in my head telling me to calm down. My heart must be beating at its fastest tempo, the thing won't slow or take a break. Sweat gathers at the back of my neck and I can feel it slowly drip down my spine.

"He doesn't let you go anywhere by yourself." The man chuckles. "He's a protective bastard, hmm?" The man looks at me expectantly, as if I should agree with him.

I do. My husband is a protective bastard. He's manipulative and ruthless and out for blood. But I will not tell this stranger, this enemy, about my husband. There's a weird feeling settling in my chest. I want to live, more than anything at this moment, I want to walk out of this dingy place alive. But I won't do it by betraying Gian.

I don't know what my captor wants. And the panic racing through my head won't let me ask, but I know that I'm meaningless in this game of chess. Gian won't come to save me, and especially not after I requested a divorce.

I'm his property, sure, but I'm not required for his success. If anything, having a dead wife will be better for him, get him sympathy. He can wait years before marrying again, just milking the dead wife card until there's nothing left.

Whatever the man in front of me wants, he won't get.

I should open my mouth, spill everything I know about *La Famiglia* to save myself. My father was a prick, taking down his beloved family wouldn't bother me at all. And even though the idea of hurting Gian stings my heart, I think I could betray him.

But then I think of Gemma, her family is so entangled in the mafia. Any detail I slip could ruin her life, could kill her loved ones. And Giuseppe, I can't deny that the man has been a better father to me than my own. I couldn't do anything to hurt him. And deep down, I know I don't want to betray Gian either. My conversation with Gemma on my wedding day flashes through my mind. Deep down, he's a good person, at least his sister thinks so. And maybe he is, maybe I haven't given him a chance to redeem himself fully.

"What do you want?" I finally speak and my voice comes out broken and rough. The lack of water has dried out my mouth, making it difficult to speak.

The laugh that leaves his mouth is sadistic, verging on a growl. "What do I want?" he repeats, his voice rough and harsh. "I want your fucking husband to pay." His fingers tighten into a fist when he speaks, his anger radiates from him. I can see it in the straight line of his lips and the twitching vein in his neck.

I don't know what Gian did to this man, but whatever it was, it clearly pissed him off. "What did he do?" I ask, curiosity taking over. And I know the longer he talks, the longer I stay alive.

A harsh growl leaves his lips at my question and he lifts a hand to run it through his sparse hair and over the days old stubble covering his jaw. His dark scowl comes eye-to-eye with me. "He ruined my fucking life."

Chapter Twenty-two

GIAN

I should pray.

That's the first thought that flashes in my mind when Rafi tells me that my wife has been kidnapped. I should pray. I should drop to my fucking knees and give the man above the clouds what he wants. I should promise to change my ways, to never kill again. Fuck it, I'll even donate to charity.

As long as Rhea walks back through that fucking door.

Underneath her hard attitude and bitchy remarks, my wife is just an innocent girl who was born to the wrong man. Had she never met her father, her life would have been completely different. Had she never met me… no one would have kidnapped her.

"Do you..." I trail off, barely able to finish the question. "Do you know who did it?"

Rafi scrubs a hand over the back of his head. The kid is terrible at giving me the bad news. All his nerves show and he has about ten tells. The shiftiness and the head touching are only two of them. "Yeah, boss." He mutters.

"Spit it out," I growl at him, I'm standing now with my fingers gripped around the edge of my wooden desk. I was in my office at the pizza shop when Rafi came to tell me the news.

"You know that agent... the one who got fired..."

The bald head of the FBI prick comes to mind. Aaron Baldwin. A long breath releases between my lips. "Fuck."

"I think he knows it was you who set him up, boss. Andrew saw his face before he shot him." Rafi heaves a breath.

Andrew. Fuck. The man is a loyal soldier, one of the reasons I put him in charge of Rhea's safety in the first place. If he dies, that will be two more deaths on my conscience.

"Where is he?" I ask.

"Surgery," Rafi responds. "He called me first," he adds. "Gave me as much information as possible before he passed out."

I scrub a hand down my face. Andrew's loyalty is as strong as I could ever ask for, if anything happens to him I'll make sure his mom and sisters are cared for. They'll want for nothing.

"How bad?" I ask.

Rafi winces. "Bad." He clears his throat, another tell of his nervousness. "There were a bunch of casings at the scene, looks like Andrew and Baldwin were shooting around the Escalade. As far as I can tell, Andrew is the only one who got hurt." He swallows hard. "Andrew said Rhea was knocked unconscious before the shoot-out. I don't think she's hurt, boss"

"Badly, you mean." His eyes go wide at my statement. "You don't think she was hurt badly."

Rafi swallows hard before nodding. "Yeah, I don't think she was shot, nor was Baldwin."

"Did Andrew get an ID on the car he was driving or anything that will help us catch the man?"

He wrings his fingers, avoiding eye contact. "No."

A ragged breath passes through my lips as I dip my head, trying to think. My head is buzzing. The uncertainty surrounding the lives of my wife and one of my best men is making me uneasy. I should have put more men on Rhea or made her stay home. She doesn't need to leave the house to do her job. I could have set up a home office for her or installed more security at my father's office.

I should have done more to keep her safe.

But she wouldn't have let me do all that anyway. My wife is too independent. She can barely stand being chauffeured around, any more security, and she would have fought me.

Would dealing with her hatred be worth saving her life?

Red tinges the edge of my vision and heat flashes through my body. I can't protect this woman, I can't protect anyone. Everyone I love, everything I've built, is on the verge of crumbling around me. I can't keep anyone safe.

I surely couldn't keep my mother safe. Her body was littered with bullets in the back of a Town Car meant for my father. There used to be an unwritten rule in *La Famiglia* that women and children were never to be harmed, but slowly we've chipped away at that ideal, and those outside of our circles were happy to toss that rule aside and hit us where it hurts the most.

Images of my father hunched over my mother's casket explode in my memory. I had never seen the man cry before that day. My father was a wisecracker, always had a joke to say to lighten the tension around us. He was good at easing nerves, that's what made him excel as a consigliere. He would get men loose, secrets would spill, and then he could analyze the situation and create a plan.

But the day of my mother's death, the man I had come to idolize was a broken piece of himself. On his knees sobbing before the body of his dead wife. I never wanted to be like that. I never wanted to love someone enough that their death would break me, shatter my world into a million pieces. I'd watched too many people go through that. Massimo lost his son, my friend Vinny lost his father. Each of them broke with the news, letting it devour them until they couldn't stand on their own two feet anymore.

I promised myself in each of these moments that I would never be like that.

I would never be unsteady in the face of tragedy because I

would never love someone enough to let it break me.

But here I am. My fingers tightened around the edge of my desk while I fight to breathe. Memories of Rhea's dark hair and bright emerald eyes envelop me and I want to let my body sink to the floor. I want to let all the emotions building inside my chest tumble out.

My breath leaves my body in uneven pants, choking me on the way out.

This is a new feeling for me, the panic has never bubbled up in my chest like this before. I've always had a handle on it, always had it under control. But I can't control this, can't get a grip around my feelings as they all swarm through my head.

"Boss?" Rafi asks, but his voice sounds far away, too distant.

I don't even recognize what's happening as my knees hit the dirty carpeting of my office, my chest caves, and I lean forward, letting my fists hit the floor in succession.

I am a failure.

Everyone I love is about to die, and everything I've built is about to crumble.

All because of me.

Gemma sets a cup of tea in front of me. I asked for coffee, but my little sister refused to appease my caffeine addiction. She's convinced I'm having a panic attack and chides me, commenting that caffeine won't help.

Despite all the tension between my sister and me, I can see the way she looks at me. Worry coats her features and I'm not sure if it's more for me or Rhea. She slides into the chair next to me at the dining room table. She was the first to arrive here, my father on her tail.

Gio's paranoia reached a record high when I called him. His first reaction was to check on Annie and the baby, and I can't say I blame him. Having a child and a marriage, one based on love and not convenience, changed my brother. He's still loyal, my most trusted advisor and soldier. But his priorities shifted. Booze left the list entirely. Since Gabriella's birth, I rarely see him with a drink, instead, he's working or with his family. He cherishes that little girl in a way I never imagined.

I wonder if I would change like that too. If Rhea popped out a small wrinkly baby, would my priorities shift? Would I suddenly become a family man?

The thought of having children makes my heart ache harder. The idea of having more things I love in this world, more things that could be taken away from me.

"Breathe," Gemma demands, slicing through the thoughts running wild in my head like a knife. "Whatever you're thinking, whatever you're beating yourself up about, it will not help you find her." Her brown eyes stare at me with wide attentiveness, her lips are pressed thin. She talks to me in a serious tone, her words slow and strong. My little sister has somehow shed her emotions and become the anchor of this family, picking up where I'm failing. Her soft hand comes to my forearm, steadying me with her touch. "You can do this, Gian. I've known you my entire life and I've never seen you let anything, anyone, get to you like this. You love her, hmm?"

Her words stop me in my tracks.

Do I love Rhea?

No, this marriage was an arrangement, a transaction. It was meant to give me strength, to make me look good to the older men in *La Famiglia*. Our relationship isn't built on love, there's no affection between us.

But those green eyes, the way they looked at me that night on the carousel when I told her about my mother, about our trips to that same attraction. It was the same look she gave me the night of our wedding. She understands me in a way that no one else does. Without the words ever being spoken, we just knew. There was always an eerie similarity between the two of us. Both missing a parent. Both trying to be the strongest in the room.

Did I love her?

I feel something for her... Appreciation, maybe? For the way she opens up those red-painted lips, wrapping them around the shaft of my cock and taking me in like it's the sweetest thing she's ever tasted. Adoration, for her cooking, for the smells of butter and garlic that I've grown to love coming home to.

Hearing her voice has become the highlight of my nights. The sweet melodic sound of her singing in the kitchen while she stirs a bubbling pot of red sauce. I've grown to enjoy my life with her, even without voicing it.

Do I love her?

Am I in love with her?

Yes.

I think I fucking love Rhea Estella Cabrera, and I won't stop until I get her back. And once I have the raven-haired beauty back in my arms, I promise I'll never let her go.

I have myself pulled more together when Christopher barges through my front door unannounced. "You fucking asshole!" he growls once he sees me, his boots stomping against the tiled floors of the entryway. Mud stains the white tiles behind him, and if my mother were alive, she'd have no problem scolding him for the action, her finger wagging in the air while she shouted.

Gemma jumps from her seat before me or my father. My hand reaches for the gun at my waist, my fingers slipping against the cool metal. The only thing stopping me from shooting the asshole for barging in and shouting as if I'm not the head of this family is the fact that Rhea loves her half brother. The last thing I want is for her to come home to another body to bury.

"Calm down," my father tells him, rising from the chair slowly, showing his age. He dusts off his navy dress slacks and gives Christopher a stern look. "We have men searching for your sister, we'll find her."

Christopher's eyes bounce from my father to me, the orbs are darker than his sisters but his hair is that same raven black, falling over his head in long locks. He needs a haircut, maybe a shave too. I'm not intimidated by her brother, by his mediocrity. He's never been someone to fear, growing up in the shadow of his father's sad success. Joe's always been a good earner, and Christopher followed after him, striking up his own racket and bringing in piles of cash. But it was never amazing, never overly successful. The kid never worked his ass off like I did. He was lazy, expected success and power to be handed to him.

He bares his teeth as he prepares to speak. The anger radiates from him. "If you get my sister killed, I'll—"

"You'll what?" I speak now. I don't stand from my seat, instead I lean back, feigning an act of callousness. I don't want him to see my emotions, the way they're swirling in my head and driving me mad. I don't want to be like him, a man who lets his feelings drive his actions.

I've always been better than that. Better trained, better at restraining myself. My success comes from my ability to step back and analyze my situations. Those who act with emotion always fail.

They always get hurt in the end.

I'm not a loser, and I refuse to let myself become one.

"What will you do?" I ask him, a cold smile playing on my lips.

Pink lips press thin. He catches himself now, realizing that he was just about to threaten his boss, not just his sister's husband. "Sorry," he mutters, lacking the formality of calling me by any name of respect.

Gemma's mouth pops open into a perfect O shape before she quickly closes it, tugging her lip between her teeth.

"What?" I ask her, my voice sterner than I mean, but Christopher's presence grates at my nerves. I don't have a good reason for being annoyed with the man. I've just never liked him or his father, and his relationship to my wife hasn't increased his charm.

"He's just worried about Rhea, same as us," Gemma whispers, the lines of her mouth twist to frown with concern.

I forgot for a moment how close my sister and my wife are. I was so wrapped up in my own worry, my own anxiety over my failures, that I forgot that there are others who love her too. My lips twitch but I will them not to show my realization, not to let the emotions show while Christopher is in our presence. He may be Rhea's brother and a made man, but my trust is stretched thin these days and he's not in my inner circle.

I wave my hand in a dismissive gesture. "It's fine," I say, bringing my gaze back to Christopher. "We're all heated."

He bows his head in a thankful gesture. "I want to find her," he says.

"Me too," I tell him, as if it even needs to be said. "And I will. Now, please leave."

Wide dark eyes flash to mine, his lip curls with anger and red rises from beneath his skin to coat his cheeks. "I can help," he says, a matter of fact.

"No," I tell him, my words concise, not leaving any room for interpretation. "You can't."

A loud huff leaves his throat, but he spins on his heel, only giving me one last dirty look as he heads for the door. "I'll find her myself," he growls, letting the door slam on his way out.

Gemma's shoulders shake as the chandelier rattles from his action. "Jesus," she mutters.

Gio walks through the door before any of us have even exhaled after Christopher's exit. My brother softly lets the door click shut as he walks toward the table we've all gathered around. "Was that Christopher who just left?" His deep eyes crinkle with concern.

"Yeah." I sigh, releasing a long breath through my lips.

Gio's eyebrows draw together as his hand comes to scrub over his chin. "I have something to tell you…" he says. "And you're not going to like it."

Chapter Twenty-three

RHEA

A sharp slap stings my cheek. The flesh there is raw and red, aching from the repeated slaps. In the hours I've been tied to this metal chair in a dank warehouse, I've learned a lot about my captor.

He's not as focused or calculated as my husband. His hand twitches when I don't answer his questions, and he sighs heavily every time he's forced to hurt me. He doesn't get off on the abuse, at least not like my father.

Joe loved to hurt me, to slap, and punch, and kick. He never flinched, never sighed. He could rattle off an entire speech while his fists rained down on me. A whole dialogue about how everything was my fault, how I did this to myself. That I deserved

My captor doesn't tell me I deserved this, doesn't insult me or my character. His focus is solely on my husband. His whereabouts, where he keeps things, does he have a safe, does he keep notes, what time does he get home. On and on he asks the questions.

I answer each one with as much of a shrug as I can manage in my tied position and the simple answer of 'I don't know.' He becomes more and more frustrated with each question.

"Tell me!" he demands, his shouts getting louder. This time, when I don't answer he kicks the chair he was sitting in earlier. The sound of the metal hitting the concrete floor reverberates through my bones.

My body is weak and sore. My muscles ache from the lack of movement and my skin stings from the abuse.

He's going to have to escalate tactics soon, we both know that. My silence is deafening and his current strategy isn't working. My pain tolerance is higher than he expected for a woman, thanks to years of beatings at the hands of my father.

From the look on his face, I don't think he expected this. A petite mafia wife like me should be weak and fragile, shouldn't be able to hold herself together for this long. He underestimated me, and that will be his fatal mistake.

If I can ever get out of here.

He paces around the warehouse and I take the moment to test my restraints again. Pressing against the rope and searching for any weak areas, anything loose enough to slip through. Nothing has changed, and unless I can dislocate a thumb, I'm not breaking free of these bindings.

His stomping stops me I can't see him but I can hear his boots as they slap against the concrete coming in my direction.

"Okay, bitch," he throws his first insult of the day at me. A strong hand grips onto my chin, yanking me forward against the rope that's tied tight around my chest. The action stings the fragile skin on my face while the rope bites into my chest. "This is your last chance," he growls, moving his face so it hovers over mine. Droplets of spit land on my skin and I itch to wipe them away, my fingers wiggling in their place behind my back. "Give me something to take your husband down or you won't walk out of this warehouse."

I don't *think* he'll kill me. He seems too weak, too good for that. But something has shifted in him, he's more unhinged than he was hours ago. Something is on the line for him, there's something he needs, and the more I toy around with him, the more likely he is to kill me.

I need to deescalate the situation, bring him down, give him something. I need to shift the advantage back into my court.

My mother used to tell me stories, tales about princesses and knights, stories about love and adventure. There was always a monster in the stories, an evil queen or dragon. There was always something to be slain. And once the battle was finished, the princess and prince would end up together. True love prevailed and a happily ever after was had for all.

But the monsters in real life are harder to see. They don't wear pointy hats or give evil speeches. They come in normal clothes with flesh and bones, looking just like anyone else. They have no discernable features that shout *Hey! I'm evil!*

The man in front of me with his hand gripped onto my face doesn't look sinister. He doesn't wear a shirt with the name 'bad guy' pinned to it. He looks distressed, pushed beyond any reasonable limit.

He looks broken.

"What did he do to you?" I ask, my voice coming out cracked and tired. I asked the same thing earlier and didn't get an answer, instead he left. Leaving me alone, presumably while he went to pump himself up, preparing for torture.

Something shifts in his eyes as he looks down at me. Earlier he said Gian ruined his life, and I guess my husband has the power to do so. He runs all of Providence, has all the politicians in his pocket. The entire city is corrupt, feeding into the hands of the mafia. If you go against *La Famiglia,* they'll burn you. Cut off your access to whatever feeds you, whatever you hold dear. Worst-case scenario, they kill you.

But my kidnapper is alive, his life intact. So it must be something else he took, something that gave him an identity.

"What did he take from you?" I ask, trying to zone in on whatever it is that this man is seeking revenge for.

He drops his grip on my chin, taking a step back as if I've repulsed him. His gaze lowers to his hands, looking at them as if they're covered in blood. It's not me who's repulsed him... he's disgusted with himself.

I take the opportunity to ask again. "What did he do to you?"

His eyes flash back up to me and his throat bobs as he swallows. "He took everything from me." He swallows. "I don't know how... but I know it was him."

"What happened?" I asked, trying to keep him talking. The more he talks, the longer I'm alive, the longer I don't have his hands on me.

"This kid... this kid ended up dead, had my fingerprints all over his apartment, but I had never been there, never even met the kid." His eyebrows squish together as he recalls the event. "I didn't do it," he says. "I didn't kill the kid, but the evidence..." he trails off.

"It was planted?" I ask.

His head bobs in response. "I don't know how." He shakes his head, anger bubbling back up to the surface. "It was overwhelming, the evidence. They took my badge, my gun, my whole reputation down the drain. And now, I'm going to be tried for murder."

His badge... "What... what agency?" My mouth feels like it's been stuffed with cotton, the dryness coats my tongue as I ask the question.

His eyes flash back up to mine when he speaks. "FBI."

Why in the world would Gian fuck around with the FBI, why would he ruin this man's life?

The monster starts to shift, changing from a scary figure in front of me into an innocent man. And the innocent man who's been hurt like me.

I drag in a ragged breath.

Images of Gian flash through my head. He's manipulative but caring. Brutal, but soft. Is it possible for the man to be both the hero and the villain of my story?

"You were..." I don't even have the full sentence out before he nods.

"I was assigned to mafia activity in Providence. Gian DelGado takes over the city and I start following him, thinking there's no way this guy can be above the law, he has to slip up sometime." He exhales, running a hand through his thin hair. "I got close," he says. "Really fucking close. I got two men to flip," he laughs softly. "Practically unheard of, having two informants. I was about to be promoted, all I needed to do was take that asshole down. But he got me first." He pants. "I guess this is what I get for trying to be the good guy, for following the law." His voice rises as he speaks now, the anger replenishing itself. "A fucking murder charge."

I latch onto one thing from his rant.

He has two rats in Gian's organization.

Chapter Twenty-four

GIAN

Gio scrubs a hand over his jaw, raking through the days of stubble as he relays his news. Charlie, one of his men, was having drinks at the club when he ran into someone from Christopher's crew. This guy says Christopher has been unhinged lately, acting all funny, asks if Charlie knows anything. Charlie says no, but asks what he means. The kid tells him that Christopher is barely at the worksite anymore, doesn't answer his phone, he's been acting sketchy. And then last week, a gray sedan pulls up to the sight with some suit in it and Christopher freaks out on this guy, jumps in the car and they can see him yelling and stuff, when he gets out he's shouting at the man telling him to never show up here again.

Gio's eyes find mine as he wraps up the story. "I have this

crazy suspicion," he says. "You know how that FBI agent showed up at the pizza shop and told you your ship isn't tight?" My brother is the only one I told about that incident, the only person I trust enough to know that we have a second leak, someone else talking about our business to the Feds. "What if Christopher was meeting with Agent Baldwin?"

Your ship is not tight.

The words ring in my head.

I already killed Silvio, I already took care of the leak in my ship.

"What if Silvio wasn't the only rat?" Gio says, speaking my mind.

"You think Christopher's a rat?" Gemma asks, her features twisted in confusion. "What does that have to do with Rhea being kidnapped?"

Fuck.

"Christopher. This is all him."

My father and Gemma stay home, working my father's IT contact to track down Rhea's location by tracking her phone.

Gio drives with me to Rhea's family home. Christopher is MIA. We couldn't find him at his apartment, construction site, or his local bar. He has a close relationship with Elena, that much I know from Rhea, so we head over to the Cabrera family home next.

I can practically taste the blood on my lips. I make no promises about what will happen tonight. One wrong move and it's likely that both Cabrera men will die, and I can guarantee that both Cabrera women will only be sad about one of them.

Joe's a lot of things, a terrible father, a shitty husband, and a huge ass. But the one thing he's not is a traitor.

But his son is.

Still, I'd much prefer an asshole over a traitor.

Christopher won't live to see tomorrow. There's no way I can let it happen, no way I can allow a rat to live in this organization.

This life requires an oath, one sealed with blood and fire. One that is meant to last, to take all our secrets to the grave.

Christopher talking to the Feds is a betrayal of that oath. It's bad enough to break his promise, to turn his back on his brothers, but to talk to the FBI is the worst sin. And the one sin that's unforgivable in this life is turning rat.

Elena is the one to answer the door. Her face is healed, the bruises almost disappearing, just the faintest yellow remaining on her skin.

She's surprised when she sees me. Immediately her spine straightens and I can see her slip her mafia wife mask into place. Her mascara is smudged just the slightest, a small run dripping to her cheekbone. When she catches my eyes there, her fingers lift to wipe under her eyes.

"Come in," she says, in the fakest cheerful voice she can muster, opening the door wider.

Elena and Joe were my next call after finding out Rhea was

missing. As much as I can't stand the man, they deserved to know what had happened to their daughter. Joe's anger slipped on the phone. He accused me of not being able to protect her, which was the same thought rolling through my head at the moment.

He hung up hastily, not wanting to talk to me. I didn't care. I didn't want to talk to him either.

Now as I walk into his home, I see him seated at the dining room table with a cup of coffee and a cannoli placed in front of him.

"Do you want anything to drink, or eat?" Elena asks. She's wearing the mask of the good wife, trying not to show any emotions in front of me, but I can see the cracks in her façade. She adores her stepdaughter and having raised her for half her life, the 'step' title doesn't mean much. To her, her daughter is missing. It's probably breaking her apart inside, yet here she is making coffee and cannoli for her husband.

"No, thank you," I tell her, opening my arms so I can bring her in for a hug, using the moment to whisper softly so only she can hear. "I'm going to find her, and I'm going to bring her home." When I pull back, Elena looks up at me with glassy eyes.

"Thank you." She mouths.

Next, I go to Joe, noting there are two place settings set at the table, but just Joe sitting there. I don't want to ask if Christopher is here, as not to tip him off that I'm looking for him, but I have a sneaking suspicion that the other setting is for Christopher.

Elena scurries back to the kitchen, leaving me and Gio behind with her husband. Joe leans back in his chair, raising the mug of coffee to his lips before he acknowledges me. The sign of disrespect brings a fleck of red to my vision. But I can't expect much more from the man. He's always been an ass, and now with a rat for a son, his grave has practically been dug.

"So," he says. He still hasn't stood, offered me a seat or addressed me as boss. I let the strikes tally in my mind, adding them up as justification for when I kill him later.

"So," I repeat, smoothing my hands down my blazer. I don't have much to say, much to ask. I want to keep him on edge for a moment.

Before he responds, I hear a door open behind me and Christopher comes down the hall. He stops in his tracks when he sees me and Gio standing there.

"Gian," he says, shifting on his feet. "What are you doing here?"

"Just wanted to come to talk about your sister. See if you heard anything. Have you heard anything, Chris?" I pinch my eyebrows as I ask the question.

The anger has dropped from Christopher. I don't think he expected Gio and I to show up here. He looks shifty and anxious as he tucks his hands into his pockets. "No," he says. "I haven't heard anything since Dad called me this morning to say she was missing."

"So you don't know where she is?" I ask. it's clear from the tone of my voice that I think he knows something, but I don't outright accuse him.

The two thick caterpillars of his eyebrows pinch together as he lifts his hands, shrugging. The gesture is too forced, too fake. "I don't know anything," he says.

I dip a finger through the cannoli cream at the place setting I'm sure is Christopher's, bringing the ricotta mixture to my lips, for no reason other than to piss him off. "That's good." I smile. "Rhea makes them just the same, must've learned from Elena."

Christopher's gaze darts between my brother, Joe, and myself. He's trying to hide the concern, trying to push it down by wringing his fingers and reading the room. But I can see it. There's sweat pooling at his temples, threatening to drip down the sides of his face. He's shifting between his two feet, the uncertainty of his future manifesting itself into fidgeting legs and fingers.

"Nothing you want to tell me?" I ask him again, letting that wicked smile rest on my face. "Nothing at all?"

Christopher swallows hard, his neck bobbing with the action.

"Nothing like why you're a rat? Or why your little sister is now in the hands of the man you turned rat to?"

His face pales at my accusation, the color rushing from his cheeks.

"Gian…"

"Save it." I interrupt.

"Now hold on…" Before Joe even has his feet under him to stand up, Gio whacks him with the butt of his gun, sending him back into his chair and tipping it over. He falls to the floor, his hand clutching his head.

Elena runs to the dining room, stopping in her tracks when she hits the doorframe. Her eyes flicker over to her husband on the floor, the gun in my brother's hand, and her son standing with his hands up.

I give her a softer look, not the menacing smile I was just using on her son. "Elena," I say, "I need you to go upstairs and be patient while I work on bringing your daughter home."

She looks between me and her son's back, tears brimming her eyes. "Gian," she breathes.

"Everything's going to be okay," I assure her before she can finish whatever sentence was on the tip of her tongue.

With a small nod, she turns, leaving me alone with her husband and son.

Christopher blows out a breath, opening his mouth to speak before the look on my face causes him to promptly shut his lips.

"I want two things. And two things only, no discussion, no crying, just two things. Can you do that for me?"

Christopher nods his head, dropping his hands to rest at his sides.

"I want you to tell me everything you know about Agent Baldwin. Every vehicle he's driven, every place you've met, every habit he has. And then while I try to use whatever information your useless brain provides, you're going to continue to sit here and tell my brother every single thing you've told the FBI. If you can do all of that without being a major fuck up, you won't die.

251

Can you do that?

He swallowed hard and

Good. Now

Chapter Twenty-five

GIAN

Christopher is weak as he recounts his meetings with Agent Baldwin. He's slumped at the table, his voice lowered as he tells me about the car he drives, where they normally meet, how Baldwin contacts him.

Anger builds in me hearing him recount how long he's been a rat, how many times he's gone behind my back to meet with the FBI. I'm mad at myself for not catching this sooner. He's put too many of my men's lives at risk. Hell, he's put my own life at risk. He's too close to me, he knows too much since my marriage with Rhea. Him and his father have been elevated in the organization, and while I've never fully trusted them, they still know far too much.

Gio's phone buzzes in his pocket and he brings it to his ear quickly. I don't know what the person on the other end of the line says, but my brother's eyes widen when he looks at me. "They found him," he says, "Warehouse on the corner of Eighth and Maple."

I stand from my seat quickly, I need to go save my fucking wife. My eyes trail over to her brother, sitting at her family's dining room table. I can't deal with him now, I need to take care of her first, make sure she's safe and alive, and then I can come back for him.

Charlie and Rafi wait in the corner for instructions, I called them as soon as we got here and found Christopher, knowing I would need back up in the event that we found Rhea before I finished with him.

"Take him to my warehouse." I instruct Rafi. "I don't want him to move or speak to anyone until I get back, understood."

"Wait a second!" Joe huffs, standing from his seat and wagging a finger in my direction. "My boy is loyal. He made a mistake, I'll take care of it." He seems to believe the stupid words that come out of his mouth.

I can't stop myself from laughing at the stupidity. His son isn't loyal, he's the exact opposite of loyal. He's a fucking rat. And no way in hell would I let Joe 'take care of it.'

"No," I say. "Rafi, take him."

Christopher whines, some sort of unintelligible cry that I don't have the patience to hear.

"Shut the fuck up," I yell, slipping the gun from the holster on my waist and pointing it at Christopher. "If you don't shut up I will blow out both of your kneecaps and drag you to the warehouse by your bloody stumps, do you understand me?"

His eyes dart between me and the gun pointed at him, before he nods his head frantically.

I turn to Joe next. "Your son is a traitor, you're not going to handle him. If you were able to handle him, we wouldn't be in this position. You do realize that your daughter has been kidnapped because of that idiot?"

Joe's mouth opens, a stupid retort on the tip of his tongue, but I don't give him a chance to spit it out. Instead, I stalk over to Christopher, whip the butt of the gun across his head. Christopher stumbles, before falling to the ground, knocked out cold. I can't stand either of the Cabrera men, and I surely don't have the tolerance to listen to them whine.

Joe's mouth snaps shut.

"You can either stay here with Nick, or you can go to the warehouse with them. Either way, you and I aren't finished here."

"I'll stay." Joe says, his voice low and filled with shame.

"Fine choice." I tuck the gun back into the holster and head for the door.

I have to go get my girl.

The warehouse Baldwin is keeping Rhea in is at the edge of the city. My father's IT guy was able to triangulate his cell phone signal to locate them.

Stupid man, I think. He must have really thought we wouldn't have figured out it was him or else he wouldn't have kept the phone on him. That, or all his brain cells left his body the minute I framed him for murder. Maybe even before that, considering how easy he made it for me to set him up.

Either way, this is ending today.

"You can't kill a federal agent." Gio tells me as we pull up to the warehouse. I pull the gun from its holster, checking to make sure it's loaded and unlocking the safety.

"He's not a federal agent anymore." I say. I'm not wrong, they let him go. Fired because he's facing murder charges. No one will care now if the dirty agent ends up with a bullet in his skull. Hell, I'll make it look like a suicide and everyone will think that guilt became too much for Agent Baldwin to handle. It was all so overwhelming he thought the only solution was to swallow a bullet.

Seems like a good plan to me.

"Let's go," I tell my brother.

This is the opposite of what Gio has been begging of me to do for months now. I'm supposed to be distancing myself, not getting my hands dirty, but here I am, gun in hand, marching into a dirty warehouse.

But I need to save her.

I brought her into this, forced her to walk down the aisle with a smile on her lips. The least I can do is save her from the crazy

FBI agent seeking revenge.

Gio peeks through the small crack in the window, looking into the warehouse to assess what we're about to walk into.

"She's in there," he whispers to me. "He has her tied to a chair in the center of the room."

"Is he in there?" I ask.

"Yes," my brother replies, squinting his eyes as he continues to look into the building. "He's there, looks like he's talking to her..." Gio trails off. "Gian, he's got a gun. He's waving it around at her."

"We need to go in there now."

"Listen," Gio holds out a hand to stop me. "I'm not saying we don't go in there, I'm just... are you sure you don't want to wait for back up?"

"I'm sure." I tell him.

I need to do this. I can't let this be the way Rhea and I end. Especially after everything I've done to her. And not after she asked me for a divorce. I need to fix this and I can't do that if she's dead.

"On three," he says. He counts down slowly and on three we pull open the doors, each of us entering the building with our guns raised.

Agent Baldwin's eyes widen when he sees us. He fumbles with the gun in his hand, trying to get his fingers in the right place to shoot it, but I don't wait to give him the chance.

I don't wait for him to say something mean. For him to divulge his evil plan.

I see the scared look on his face and I shoot. Letting the bullet fly from my gun and pierce his chest.

Rhea screams and Agent Baldwin flies backward. His back hits the cement floor with a loud thud. My ears ring from the gunshot and Rhea's whimpers. I run to her, letting my feet slam against the floor as I move toward my wife. Gio tosses me a knife to cut Rhea's bindings as he goes for Agent Baldwin's body, checking to see if his heart is still beating and his lungs are still pumping oxygen.

Rhea is sobbing as I cut her free from the ropes that hold her in place. As soon as her arms are free, she wraps them around me, tucking her head in the crook of my neck. I can feel her tears melt into my skin, dripping down my shirt. I finish cutting the ropes and I wrap my arms around her, bringing her into my embrace and rubbing soft circles on her back.

"Shh, baby, it's okay. You're safe now."

I look to my brother who stands up, moving away from the agent's body. He gives me a shake of his head. The man is dead.

It's all over now.

I think Rhea's in shock. Guilt nips at me as I leave her at my father's house with a handpicked selection of enforcers and my sister. I know my father will take care of her, keep her safe while I'm gone, but there's a part of me that wants to be the one that stays with her. Keep her wrapped safely in my arms.

"You don't have to be the one to take care of him, ya know." My father tells me, each of his hands pressed firmly on his hips.

I don't. I know that. I could easily have Gio take care of Christopher or Rafi or any one of my men. But it should be me.

I can't force any of my men to kill a brother, someone they worked alongside for years. This job belongs solely to me, I have to take care of it.

"I know," I tell my father.

Gio drives me to the warehouse where Christopher is being kept in silence. It's never easy having to kill one of my own, regardless if they're a traitor or not.

And this one is even harder. I can't get the image of Rhea tied to that metal chair out of my mind. Her cheek was bright red, her lip split.

She was in that mess because of her brother, the traitor who spilled our secrets to the FBI, but also because of me. I antagonized the agent and ruined his career. I shouldn't be surprised that I pushed the man toward a path of retribution.

Christopher is tied to a metal chair when I get to the warehouse, and the similarity between where he is now to where his sister was not too long ago isn't lost on me.

His forehead drips with sweat as I approach him.

The begging begins immediately, as soon as his eyes land on mine, his lips begin to move. "It was an accident." He spews. "I swear, boss, it will never happen again. Please…"

I release my gun from the holster on my waist, bringing it

up and pressing it against his temple while he sobs. I block out the fountain of words that spew from his lips. Excuses, promises, everything under the sun.

My forefinger presses down on the trigger and the bullet slices through his skin, spraying blood back, flinging droplets of red liquid onto my suit.

"No!" Joe Cabrera enters with Nick on his heels. His boots thump against the warehouse floor as he runs toward his son, crouching in front of his lifeless body.

I wonder if he would have run like that for Rhea, crouched in front of her body and wailed like a baby.

It doesn't matter.

For the third time today I raise the muzzle of my gun, lining it up with the back of Joe's head and shooting before he has the chance to turn and spew his nonsense at me.

He wasn't a rat, but he was something equally bad.

The sight of the bruises coloring his wife's skin still lingers in my mind. I didn't need Rhea to say the words to know he did the same thing to her. Painted her body in black and blue, and for what reason? Because she was a woman? Because she was physical evidence of his sins?

It didn't matter anymore.

The only thing that matters now is that she's safe.

Chapter Twenty-six

RHEA

"Where is he?" I ask Gemma for what feels like the millionth time.

The time on the clock reads midnight, and though I can't remember what time it was when Gian carried me through the doors of his family home, I know it was a while ago.

Gemma ran me a hot shower and gave me a change of clothes, she poured me an overflowing glass of wine and sat on the floor with me while I cried. Giuseppe lingers in the corner of the room, watching us and checking his phone often.

They won't tell me where Gian is.

Every time I close my eyes I see the spray of blood as it enters Agent Baldwin's chest. I see his eyes roll to the back of his head while his body falls to the floor in a lifeless heap of skin and bones.

I can't sort out my feelings.

My wrists are raw where the man had secured them together with a rough rope, but still for some reason I can't help but to think of him as a victim in this story.

My husband swung open the door to the warehouse, letting in a ring of evening light that surrounded him like a halo. He looked majestic as he came for me, bullets flying from the gun in his hand.

He saved my life.

But he also took someone else's.

Is it possible for the man to be both the hero and the villain of my story?

Both my savior and my monster?

Gian never pretended to be a god guy, he never lured me in with false promises or sweet words. From the second I met the man, I've known exactly who he is.

So why am I sitting here now, letting my mind run in circles? I knew what I was getting into when I chose to marry him, regardless of the circumstances that led me to that decision.

My heart aches from it's constant pounding when the front door swings open and heavy footsteps fall on the tile floors. I don't realize I've jumped from my seat until I feel Gemma's hand on my shoulder, anchoring me back to the present moment.

My husband walks through the entry way with Gio on his tail. His eyes find me first, looking over my body methodically, checking for any lingering injuries.

"I'm fine." I say, my voice raspy and raw from all the crying.

He nods solemnly as he steps forward, coming toward me at a slow pace. I've never seen emotion in his eyes. The dark orbs have always been cold and calculated. The most emotion I've gotten from my husband in the months we've been married is the anger that radiated from him when I said I wanted a divorce.

Now, he looks sad, remorseful even.

He takes one more step toward me until he's practically touching me, nose to nose, and then he drops to his knees. His hands lift, grasping both of mine in his palms and bringing them to his lips for a gentle kiss. "Rhea," he murmurs, "I am so sorry."

"What are you talking about?"

His eyes are heavy when they lift to meet mine, water brims the edges of his lashes and that's how I know that something is really wrong. Gian doesn't cry. My monster, my savior, my villain—he doesn't cry.

"What happened?" I ask. Worry bubbles up in my chest frantically. "What happened, Gian?"

"Your brother." He swallows hard. "Christopher is dead."

The cemetery feels cold and desolate, even though there's a crowd of people gathered around the two coffins as they're lowered into the ground. We buried them side by side in the Catholic graveyard. I can't help but laugh thinking about it.

How would God feel about the two murderers being lowered

into his ground?

My fingers trace over the cross that dangles from my throat. My death toll is up to three now. My mother, my father, my brother. Elena sobs as they lower the two caskets, her hand grips around my arm. She hasn't stopped crying since Gian gave her the news.

The boss of Providence lowered himself before my stepmother, bowing his head as he gave her the news. I thought she was going to slap him, yell, or something.

He killed her son. The child that she brought into this world and raised was gone, his life taken away.

I struggled to reconcile what he did before his death with the understanding that I would never see him again.

I couldn't separate the small boy who took me into this family from the man who betrayed me. My heart was shattered into pieces, my will to live shredded.

Gian waited on me hand and foot. Constantly checking on me, feeding me, taking care of me. He meant well, he did, and I understood his reasoning, but my heart was still broken.

My brother was still dead.

"Joseph and Christopher Cabrera were loved…" The priest reads off his prepared paper and I wonder how he can stomach saying the words. He knew them, he knew the type of men they were. They were loved, sure. But they weren't good guys.

Gian gives my hand a reassuring squeeze. I guess my husband isn't much of a good guy either, and yet here I am.

I wait for the service to end, for everyone to finish patting my shoulder and shaking my hand. People file out of the graveyard, by tomorrow morning my brother and father will no longer be on their minds. Instead, they'll only be thought of in fleeting memories triggering a quick "oh how sad" reaction before they move on.

But my head won't let them go.

My brother haunts my thoughts. His smile ingrained into my head, playing on loop.

The first time I met Christopher, he walked into my room, a hesitant look on his face. Joe was downstairs screaming at Elena for something or other. It was my first night after my mom passed, my first night not in my normal bed. Instead, I was in a stuffy guest room that has just been dubbed mine, but nothing in the room resembled me.

Christopher shoves his hands in the pockets of his jeans, the tail of his Patriots jersey getting ruffled with the action. "Hey," he whispered. "I'm sorry about your mom."

I didn't respond. Not because his empathy didn't seem sincere. I could see the emotion in his eyes, the sorrow that pooled in those brown orbs. "Mine is pretty cool," he said, "I can share her."

I didn't speak. I never did in those first few months after she died.

But Christopher didn't care. He sat down next to me on the guest bed and continued to talk. Words rained from his lips. He told me about football, about the kids he hung out with at school.

265

He told me about how bad he was at math.

He filled every inch of silence, transporting me from the grief that surrounded me into his own little world.

I had no right to be loved by him.

I was the wicked stepsister, the mistress's baby. He should have hated me, should have picked on me and wanted me gone.

But that sweet boy, that innocent eleven year old boy took me into his home and loved me. Protected me.

I messed up.

Those were his last words to me before I ran away from him, leaving him behind in that coffee shop.

His actions were wrong. He fucked up. But he wanted to protect me, the way he always had.

My chest feels like it's caving in as a sob wrecks my body.

"Rhea," Gian's arm snakes around my waist, holding me up.

Suddenly, I'm back in the graveyard, standing over my brother's coffin. Men stand off to the side, shovels in their grip. They're waiting for me to be done so they can cover the metal casket with dirt, seal him into this plot to never be seen again.

I can't help the tears that drain from my eyes, coating my lashes and my cheeks, dragging my mascara down with them.

"Where's Elena?" I mutter to my husband, letting him pull me further into his arms until I'm enveloped in his warmth.

"Gio took her."

Elena has been a wreck since the news. To Gian's credit, he's done nothing but take care of her. Posting men at her house to fulfill her every need. Considering he's the one who took her son from this world, he's awfully kind to her.

"Are you ready to go?" he asks, his voice softer than I've ever heard him. He's gentle with me lately, tiptoeing around me like I'm fragile. Like I might break at any moment.

"Yes," I whisper.

I let him lead me from the gravesite and into the black Escalade that waits on the road. Rafi drives us, Andrew is at home recovering from the bullet that pierced his arm. My heart aches when I think about him taking a bullet for me.

There are days when I hate the business my husband runs, hate the company he keeps. But the men he surrounds himself with are loyal, they have each other's backs. My brother just wasn't one of them.

I can't say I hate the mafia, I just hate what it took from me.

Chapter Twenty-Seven
RHEA

It's been three weeks since I buried my brother.

Four weeks since my body was tied to a metal chair in a dank warehouse. Four week since my brother was shot in the head and my father taken down with him.

Four weeks and one day since I let my husband fuck me on a carousel.

I keep track in my head. Mentally counting down every day, marking every day I'm alive as a success.

Bridget Montgomery walks into my office following closely behind Gemma. "Hi," I tell the petite blonde hair girl, extending my hand for her to shake.

She looks scared in front of me, she fidgets with her purse and her eyes dart around the room.

"Giuseppe will be here in a moment," I tell her. "He's agreed to take your case, no charge." I assure her.

Giuseppe never takes cases like this, but for me, he's made an exception. Most likely because most of my family is dead and I'm still married to his son, but I don't argue. I won't lie to myself and believe that Giuseppe is the type of attorney I wanted to be when I grew up. I thought the law was a pristine place, that justice serves all. But I realized along the way that you have to be a little dirty if you want to win.

And Giuseppe is that.

He skates the edges of the law, manipulating it in order to win. Most of the time, it's for the bad guys. But who's to say we can't use his powers for good?

"Ms. Montgomery," Giuseppe greets, entering the office with his hand extended. "Nice to meet you," he tells her, "Now let's talk about getting you justice."

Bridget is in the office for over an hour before Gemma finally escorts her out. Her story makes me want to scream. The desire to burn the world down fills my body. How is it even possible for so much bad to exist in this world?

"Ya know," Giuseppe breaks my chain of thoughts. "When your father asked me to hire you, I never anticipated it to lead here."

I snort. I'm sure none of us did. He would have never intertwined me with this family if he knew it would be his downfall.

"I can't say I'm mad about it though," Giuseppe adds. "I know you're hurt." He reaches out, taking my hands into his own. "You have every reason to be. But you're stronger than I anticipated, hell, I think you're stronger than anyone's anticipated." He chuckles for a moment, "You brought my son to his knees, and I don't think anyone saw that coming."

I can't help but to smile at that. Gian DelGado, the King of Providence, the asshole who thought everyone should bow to him. Giuseppe wasn't wrong. Months ago, I would have never guessed that Gian would kill for me, that he would take out his own men and the FBI to protect me.

"You're more than just his *wife,*" Giuseppe continues. "You're a smart woman. You do a good job here, I'd keep you here forever, but I know that's not what you want." He smiles softly. "So go pass that test, and then we'll set up your own practice. I'd like you to run it out of this office, with me, but I understand if you want a cooler place." He chuckles.

"Giuseppe—" I start to interrupt him but he waves a hand to stop me.

"Just," he sighs heavily. "I always wanted my sons to take after me, ya know? All old men think like this, we all want a legacy. My sons have their heads elsewhere, and that's fine, but you... you, Rhea, are going to be a great lawyer, and I'm proud to have you as a daughter." His eyes twinkle with the faintest trace of water filling his lower lash line.

I never had a father figure.

271

My mother was notoriously single after her venture with my father, and I never considered Joe to be a real father. I think real fathers have to care about you to even be considered for that title.

But Giuseppe? I can feel his love radiating from him.

"Thank you," I tell him, my own eyes filling with tears. "I would love that."

Gian's arms slip around me while I knead dough on the marble countertop. He's been gentle with me lately, far more gentle than he was in the beginning. He's changed for me. When we met, he wanted to own me, to make me his.

I don't see that side of him anymore.

"What are you making?" He whispers, his breath coasting over the crook of my neck.

"Homemade noodles." I tell him, rolling the ball of dough and pressing it down with my palm.

"Mm-hmm." The vibration of the noise radiates through me. "When will they be ready?"

"The dough needs to rest first. Grab me the plastic wrap." He complies, grabbing the roll and pulling off a piece of plastic for me. I wrap the dough tightly in the clear material and stick it in the fridge for later.

"So, we have time then?"

I laugh, dusting the flour from my hands. "For what?"

He moves in closer to me, pressing my body back against the counter and caging me in. "We never revisited your request."

"My request?"

His lips come to the crook of my neck, kissing, and sucking gently. "You asked me for a divorce."

"Oh," my stomach drops.

My divorce comment feels like it was made ages ago. I barely remember who I was when that word left my lips.

"Gian,"

"No, *cara*. Let me talk, hmm?"

I press my lips together, nodding at him silently to continue.

"I don't do love. I don't put my heart into other people because it gives them too much power. People leave. People can hurt you, so I don't give them the chance. But I put my heart into you, or maybe it's that somehow you snuck into mine. And mine was well guarded." He slaps a hand to his chest. "I don't know how you did it, Rhea Estella Cabrera, but when I thought something had happened to you I wanted to die. I would rather die than be without you. That's how fucked you've made me. You wiggled your way into my life and now I can't be without you. I want to give you a divorce, because I want to give you whatever you want. But I'm a selfish man, *cara,* and I don't want to let you go. But I won't trap you, I won't do that to you. So, if you want a divorce, say the word and I will make it happen. But, Rhea, I am begging you to stay."

His words cut through me like a knife. Slicing through the icy ropes that have locked my heart up since my head hit the pavement four weeks ago.

I wasn't meant for love either.

I didn't know what a real relationship looked like. I had only ever seen my father and Elena, and their marriage was less than healthy.

I don't know what love requires, what kind of sacrifices it demands.

I don't have any idea what hardships we'll face.

There is a part of me that wants to run. A voice in my head yelling to take this out and run for the hills.

But my gut says to stay.

Gian's not perfect. He's a product of his environment. The creation of being raised in this life. But he's also his father's son and it's clear to me that the men in this family love with their whole hearts, with every fiber of their being.

I can still feel his arms wrapping around me after he released me from my binds in that warehouse. I can still see the look of pure desperation on his face when he found me.

So he's not perfect. Maybe he's not the good guy. Maybe in someone else's story he's the villain.

But he's not in mine or at least not anymore.

He's my hero, the one who cuts the ropes holding me down and brings me back into the light of day. He's the one who keeps me afloat when I feel the current about to pull me under.

"Rhea," he whispers, his fingers trailing along my jawline sending a bolt of electricity through me.

"I don't want a divorce." I whisper. "I just want you."

His lips come crashing down on mine upon hearing the words leave my mouth. The kiss is harder, more passionate than any kiss I've had from him the last month. He wraps his hands around my waist, lifting me up onto the countertop. His hands roam my body, sending sparks through me.

"I love you, Rhea." He whispers, the trail of his breath flutters over my skin.

"I love you too."

He doesn't waste anytime after my confession, he strips the thin tank top I'm wearing from my body, palming his hand over my breasts. "Let me show you how much, baby." He fingers the top of the leggings I'm wearing, pulling the elastic fabric down my legs, taking my thong with it.

My addiction comes rushing back to me as he brings his mouth to my slit. I almost forgot how much I loved the feeling of him, how desperate and needy I became for his touch.

A finger circles my entrance while his tongue begins to work on my clit, sucking the throbbing bundle of nerves. He uses my wetness to dive his finger into my cunt, pressing in and out of me at a steady pace before adding a second one. He curls the digits, finding that spot inside of me that makes me cry out.

"Give it to me, baby," he groans, his mouth glistening with my juices. "Give it all to me."

I'm a mess as he dives back in, his tongue lapping over my clit while his fingers continue their assault. "Fuck," I cry out. "Gian."

I fall over the cliff of my release with unintelligible screams and my hands fisted in my husband's hair.

He pulls me from the counter before I even have a chance to breathe, to come down from my high. He flips me over, using the palm of his hand to press my chest down onto the surface. His other hand releases him from the dress slacks he's wearing, pulling his cock free. He palms his shaft before bringing it to my opening.

"I'm addicted to this sweet pussy of yours, ya know that?" He drops his cock from his grip to slap my ass, the sound ringing through the kitchen. "All I can fucking thinking about is the next time I'm going to get you bent over for me. Do you hear that, baby? You're like a fucking drug to me. I've never been addicted to anything." He sweeps a finger through my juices, flicking my clit. "But you? I'll never get enough of you."

He presses his cock into me, stretching me as he goes. My mouth opens and my eyes roll back at the feel of him inside me.

He's not the only addict in the room. I can't get enough of him either, he feels like heaven and sin all rolled neatly into one mouthwatering package.

"Jesus," I moan.

"Nah, baby, just you and me here."

He rams into me, over and over again. My nipples press against the countertop, the surface providing a delicious friction and Gian's fingers find my clit again.

My head is hazy, somewhere above the clouds in ecstasy. Dirty words leave his lips as his breath skates over my back.

I can barely control myself, barely remember my name as I come undone around him. It feels like my whole body is releasing, everything built up in me falls away as I let go.

"Good girl," he purrs, "come on my cock, baby." He demands. I'm limp as I hear him groan, pushing his dick into me at an erratic pace. He moans a final time as I feel his seed fill me, leaking from me as he pulls back.

"Fuck," he mutters. "You're so fucking beautiful, Rhea. So fucking pretty with my cum leaking out of you."

I feel beautiful as he whispers the words, lifting me in his strong arms and carrying me back to our bathroom. I feel like a goddess in Gian's presence, with his hands on my body and his lips whispering sweet nothings into my ear.

So we're not traditional.

So we didn't find each other in a normal way.

Fuck normal.

I'll take this fucked up passionate path any day.

Epilogue
RHEA

Four Years Later

No one visits the graves of traitors.

Except for me, I guess.

I come once a month, a handful of white roses in my grip. I visit Christopher's grave first, setting out fresh flowers before I head over to my mother's. Hers is where I spend the most time. I tell her all the things she's missed.

I tell her about her grandchildren. God, she would have loved the babies. Luca was born first, my perfect dark haired little boy. He looks more like Gian than me, which I thank God for every day. I don't know if I could handle seeing my father's resemblance in my little boy. "Luca just turned three," I tell my mother. I probably look crazy, sitting with my legs sprawled across the grass, talking to a tombstone, but it brings me peace.

"Isabella is a little girly girl," I laugh. "You'd love her." Izzy came less than a year after Luca, a symptom of my husband not being capable of keeping his hands off of me.

I rub a hand over my stomach, it's not round yet, just a little bump holding our third baby. "This one's our last." I say with a laugh. After this, I refuse to have any more of Gian's children. Two felt like plenty, but the kids brought out the sensitive side of my husband and once we started, he wanted more. Plus, he claims he loves being one of three, even though Gemma refutes this claim.

I hope it's another girl. I don't think I can handle having another son to follow in Gian's footsteps and our little girls will never grow up to feel like objects. They'll never be traded for money or territory. Their marriages will never be arranged.

I trace my fingers over the cross that my mother used to wear daily, feeling the intricate details of the metal.

For a long time, I always wondered how different my life would be if she were here, if I never had met my father.

Would I still be a lawyer? Would I still have my own practice, my own non-profit seeking justice for women? I know one thing. I wouldn't be married to Gian. For a while I wished that to be true. I wanted our whole marriage to fizzle and disappear.

But then he dropped to his knees, tears in his eyes, and apologized to me.

And even though my heart broke when he told me what he

had done, I still loved him.

My hero and my villain.

I stand from the grave, dusting the stray grass off my jeans.

"Bye Mom," I tell her, blowing a kiss.

Andrew no longer drives me around. I think Gian gave him a promotion after he took a bullet for me. He still stops by often to visit Luca and Izzy, both kids affectionately refer to him as Uncle. They're blessed to have so many people who love them unconditionally.

Gian bought me a new car that I drive myself, an argument that I won. It's a shiny silver Range Rover with soft leather seats and all the bells and whistles. It takes me less than five minutes to get to Gio and Annie's house from the graveyard.

The house is filled by the time I get there. Our family and friends are spread throughout the backyard. There are sunflowers, both fake and real everywhere, and a huge "Happy Birthday Gabriella!" banner.

I can spot Luca's head of dark hair running around with Gigi, Gio and Annie's youngest daughter. She has a head of black hair and crystal blue eyes. Gemma runs after them, shouting something I don't catch. Liam, now graciously welcomed to family gatherings, sits in a chair with a grumpy Cross on his lap. Cross looks more Irish than Italian, a fact that makes Giuseppe crazy.

I find my husband with his brother, a glass of whiskey in one hand and Izzy on his hip.

If you would have told me five years ago that Gian DelGado would be a hands-on father, I would have laughed. But here he is. He presses a kiss to Izzy's head before handing her off to me.

"Mama!" My toddler coos as she snuggles into my arms. I can't help but to squeeze her and inhale the scent of her baby shampoo.

I thank heaven every day for the way our lives have turned out.

For our health and our sweet babies.

Gian grins widely at me as I hold Izzy. Our story was unconventional, our marriage was practically a fraud, but somehow this crazy life worked out for us.

Gemma runs over to us panting, the kids on her heels. "We need family photos," she smiles.

My eyes scan over the three DelGado siblings, all with their matching olive skin and heads of dark hair, each sporting a smile. We've been through so much, all six of us, but somehow in the end, we managed to find happiness.

I look to our children next, five (soon to be six) babies who don't know the legacy they've been born into yet.

I hope they do better than us.

I hope they rule the world.

Other Books

STANDALONES

Velvet Lullabies

Shattered

THE DELGADO TRILOGY

Gio

Gemma

Gian

THE SINNERS OF NEW ORLEANS

Alliance

Deception (Coming 2021)

Obsession (Comming 2022)

Birthright (Coming 2022)

About Natalia

Natalia Lourose is an author of romantic suspense, dark, and mafia romance. She attributes her obsession with bad boys and criminals to watching far too much television and reading smut as a teenager. She calls Michigan her home and lives with her husband and three fur-babies. When not writing she can normally be found on tik-tok or some form of social media.

Printed in Great Britain
by Amazon

63086195R00163